Confessions

of

Anansi

David Brailsford

LMH Publishing Limited

Cover Design; Susan Lee-Quee

Book Design, Layout & Typesetting: Michelle M. Mitchell

Published by: LMH Publishing Limited
7 Norman Road,
LOJ Industrial Complex
Building 10
Kingston C.S.O., Jamaica
Tel: 876-938-0005; 938-0712
Fax: 876-759-8752
Email: lmhbookpublishing@cwjamaica.com
Website: www.lmhpublishingjamaica.com

Printed in the U.S.A.   ISBN 976 8184-51-5

*Dedicated to all of the wonderful storytellers
who have kept Anansi alive.*

Introduction

It was late during an evening in March 2001, when I was visiting my second 'home' in Porus in the Parish of Manchester, Jamaica.

The weather was hot and sunny, a dramatic change from the miserable cold back home in England. It was so pleasant that I sat out on the verandah of Kay's house, sorting through the notes that I had made in the National Library in Kingston the previous week.

My publisher had asked me to consider writing a book about Kwaku Ananse, the legendary folk hero of Jamaica, but initially I had been apprehensive about this project, because I presumed that other authors had already explored the subject matter most thoroughly, but in trawling the book shops, I found very little material on this fascinating subject.

There was, of course, classic writing by Louise Bennett and I was fortunate to come across a monumental work by Laura Tanna, about folk story tellers in Jamaica, entitled 'Jamaican Folk Tales and Oral Histories'. The National Library contains old and rare volumes about our hero, but as I browsed the shelves in the high street book shops, new volumes about his amazing adventures were not on view, so it seemed that tales of Anansi were no longer at the centre of Jamaican culture.

I had spent the evening at my friend Dokie's bar, trying to squeeze a story or two out of the locals, but was greeted with:

"We remember being told the stories when we were young, but we don't bother with them any more."

One man even said:

"We're told in the scriptures to keep away from anything pagan."

It wasn't until later that I came to understand the association between Anansi and pagan gods.

My wife Leonie had gone to bed and apart from the sporadic barking of the neighbourhood dogs, all was quiet and still. I needed to be on the watch for the occasional marauding mosquito, but apart from this, there was little to disturb my solitary thoughts.

"Good evening, David!"

I stood up, looking out through the iron security grill into the yard, to see who would be calling at such a late hour.

No-one was there.

"Good evening, David!" I'm up here."

Frowning with confusion I looked up. A spider, as big as my fist was swinging over my head, dangling on a thread that led directly to a web in the porch ceiling.

Taken by surprise, I momentarily flinched ......not because I had any aversion to spiders, but I was startled to be confronted by one that talked and knew my name.

"I'm sorry if I made you jump, but I couldn't help but overhear you reading my stories."

I was still speechless.

"Let me introduce myself. My name is Quaku Ananse.

"But you're only a mythical folk hero!" I stuttered.

"So they say, but I can assure you that I am as real as you are."

I flopped back and my tongue was still for some moments, but when I had gathered myself I said:

"I'm very pleased to make your acquaintance Mister Anansi. I've been reading about some of your adventures, but never dreamed that we could meet in this way."

"Thank you sir! Tell me why are you so interested in my life"

I explained that his antics intrigued me, so I wished to write my book about him, but had not yet decided how to go about it.

Anansi was delighted and came down to the settee, to do a little dance beside me.

"That's wonderful! You're the answer to my prayers to Nyame."

So he talked and talked for hours and hours and I listened.

His story took me on a journey to Ghana in Africa to meet his father. Then he introduced me to his family and described their often hazardous journeys throughout Jamaica, meeting the historical heroes of the island. Every so often, he would throw in a story about the tricks that he played on his friends and enemies.

It was a magical tale, which became the inspiration for my writing about this famous character of the island.

Fancy him being real!

Anansi expressed his concern that the Jamaican people no longer told his stories, and he feared, like the fairies in Peter Pan, that if they didn't believe in him any more........ he would surely die!

Leonie woke me the following morning. I had fallen asleep out on the porch.

Babbling incoherently, I leapt to my feet and looked for my new friend, but he had gone, leaving no trace of the web behind him.

When I had recovered sufficiently, I told my startled wife the story of the midnight visit..... but she only smiled.

"Your imagination never fails to amaze me, David."

But I knew better.

The lisping voice of Kwaku Ananse still scuttered through my brain and the moment I arrived home in England, I set down this remarkable tale.

The reading matter that follows is intended for young hearted people of all ages.

Originally I believed that Anansi stories were intended only for children, but he told me how the whole family and even a whole community were often the wide eyed audiences at the narration of his cunning.

This book is therefore intended to be shared by all ages, being as it is, a micro history of the legendary heroes of the Jamaican nation and a cry for the freedom of its people.

I had been reticent to write, because I believed that I could only do Anansi justice by penning his tales in the local Jamaican patois, but I remembered the last words that Anansi had said before I fell asleep:

"David! I don't care whether you write in Patois, English, Ashanti or even Chinese, but PLEASE tell my story!"

So I will.

Enjoy!

Acknowledgements

I must thank my new friend David, for listening to my life story one night in Porus and for the subsequent effort he made to write this book about me.

To Mike Henry, the publisher, for encouraging David to seek me out.

To the National Library of Jamaica, for preserving old and precious books about my tricks and schemes.

To John Stilgoe, a talented man living in England, who has brought David's writing to life with beautiful illustrations.

I hope to meet him one day.

I asked David to thank his daughter Marie, who helps him with something that they call word processing.

A special thanks to my good friend Louise Bennett, for the great effort that she has made over many years to keep me alive.

Thank you Laura Tanna, for encouraging those wonderful storytellers to share my stories and for giving up your time to write them down.

To Jean Small, who is the tutor/co-ordinator of the Philip Sherlock Centre for the Creative Arts and a member of Jackmandora, the Storytelling Association of Jamaica. Thank you for the nice things you said about me in the Gleaner.

Thanks to everyone who still believes in me. Please keep me alive by telling your friends about me.

From time to time call out my name and I will come.

Anansi

Contents

The Confessions of Anansi 1

How I became a Spider 5

How my waist became slim 10

How Anansi tricked his father 17

Why Anansi lives in plantain trash 27

How I was tricked by Bredda Monkey 34

Why Tumble Bug rolls in the dung 41

Anansi's grave 47

Cowitch and Mr. Foolman 55

When Anansi's wife tried to leave him 63

The nine yam hills 73

Why Brer Dog sits and watches 78

When Anansi's house was in a tree 84

The problem I had with Fire 90

Brer Anansi, Tiger and Rat 95

Brer Rooster tricks Anansi 100

How Green Lizard earned his stripes 106

Tiger's bone hole 112

The sheepskin suit 120

The gungo peas 128

The Confessions
of Anansi

I'm weary and as I lay amongst the trash for shade in the yard, I fear that I may soon be dead.

It's been very hot in Jamaica today, so I'm resting here, quite exhausted, peeping out to see what happens.

Maas Alvan has been away all day, presumably working hard on his few acres, but he's just sauntered through the gate, carrying a bundle of kindling under his left arm and swinging his trusty cutlass in the other, midst a noisy outcry from the yard dogs.

"Dinner ready yet, Winnie?" he calls over to his wife, who's busy preparing the pickney for a bath.

"Won't be long!" she replies without turning her head.

With a nod Alvan puts down the wood and leaning the hard-worked cutlass against the house steps, he removes his lace-less work boots, then rubs his stubbly beard, a regular habit that always precedes a good wash. Taking off his old cap, he reveals a head of unkempt curly black hair, then prepares to wash in a bowl of cold water that has been awaiting his return. He looks down at his reflection, smiles at his weather beaten face, rubs hard at his tobacco stained teeth with his index finger, then taking a deep breath he plunges his head into the water, immediately re-emerging to make a great splutter that awakens a smile on Winnie's face.

"Mi sell all de achee on de Mandeville Road today," declares Winnie.

"Good! We need di moni."

They both work hard to feed and educate their family.

This morning I'd seen Winnie send their two daughters off to school and they'll soon be back, so she's frying up some fish bought from a travelling vendor.

They're sizzling away in a Dutch pot that's standing on an open wood fire and a smell of spices pervades the yard.

Another bowl on the porch has been standing in the sun to warm for the baby's bath. Two crossed sticks sit over the bowl, to keep the duppies or ghosts away.

Winnie's a tall, fair skinned Masai-like woman, who flaunts a large thick nose below most unusual blue eyes. The latter, along with her complexion, she inherited from great grand mother, following an unwelcome liaison with the white boss or bukra massa back in the days of slavery.

She stands, the sleeves of her white blouse rolled up to her elbows, her floral skirt flowing down to her bare feet, ready for the splashy task to come.

Her loving smile at Alvan's washing contortions, reveals that her teeth are where they can usually be found in a glass of water on the dining room sideboard. She never wears them about the house, only displaying her dentures when she goes out or when special company calls. She would never dream of having them in to eat her food.

As she's just about to wash her youngest, the two girls arrive home from school, resplendent in their light blue uniform dresses, dark blue ties and white blouses. Throwing down their satchels, they greet mother with an affectionate tug of her plaited hair.

"Put up yu arms dem," and mother carefully pulls off each white blouse, ready to wash, dry and iron for the following day. "Go get a cold drink, den go do yu work".

Oh dear! There's that cat again.

I cower down, not wishing to draw its attention, for she loves to eat the likes of me.

Why doesn't she go look for a lizard up an orange tree?

There she goes, so I can sigh with relief.

Winnie finishes bathing Nathan, then calls out:

"Cum fi yu dinner," and everyone bustles indoors.

With aching joints, I creep across the yard, climb up to the veran-dah, slip into the dining room, scale unseen up the wall and hide high up in a corner, ready to look down on the gathering.

They sit at the table and food is served.

A word of prayer is offered up and Alvan asks for a blessing from their God, who they call Jehovah.

They have forgotten Nyame.

Patiently waiting and listening, I hope to hear some mention of my name, but to no avail.

A whole evening passes, with not a single mention of Anansi.

Father informs Winnie:

"Mi a go plant corn tomorrow!"

Mother grunts in reply, then observes:

"Nathan, im not well". It appeared that he might be coming down with something.

Patrice and Geana hear none of this, but jabber on incessantly about something new at school that they call a computer.

But never one solitary word about me.

There was a time, long ago, after dinner was over, when the old folks would gather everyone around a fire outside and begin the telling of much loved tales about my outrageous adventures.

My name was known throughout Jamaica and across the sea in far away Africa, but now no-one pays me heed and many moons have passed since my name was bantered around the village. No longer am I the subject of the good humoured stories that began in Ghana, where I was born.

This makes me fearful, for I begin to wonder whether my people still believe in me.

Without their love and affection I know I will die!

For a long time now my strength has been ebbing away, so I pine, yearning for those happier times, when each day was full of exciting schemes.

Oh! To trap some gullible victim with a well thought out trick.

Resting here, I fall into an uneasy sleep, my dreams taking me back to Ghana, where I was conceived in and born from the mind of the Ashanti nation.

* * * * * *

My father is the mighty sky god Nyame and my mother is Asase Ya.

Father named me Kwaku Ananse and after he and I brought forth the sun, the moon and the stars, we set about the task of creating mankind and I taught these beings how to tend the land and grow crops of grain and they worshipped me.

Some of them, however, called me a villain, the sly and crafty one, the mischievous trickster, but this was my way of showing them how to free themselves from those who would bind them.

I taught them that by using their brains, they could outwit their enemies and be victorious over those who would persecute them.

Sometimes I appeared to them as a man, but more often I came as a spider.

In this form, I would tiptoe around their nation, tricking anyone who might try to take advantage.

I taught my people that one could survive in times of tribulation by 'working brains' or cunning, and that crafty tricks could often help the weak to triumph over the strong.

My name has been spelled and said in many ways, from Anancy to Anante, from Hanansi to just Nancy by my friends. Sometimes 'Brer' is put before my name, like my cousin Brer Rabbit, who lives in a land to the west and north.

Later, they called me Spider man.

How I Became A Spider

Listen to my story!

This tale makes me smile, for it does nothing for my reputation as one who is always supposed to be successful with plots and scheming. But tell it I must, for in it you will see why I came to be called Spider man.

I was well known around the district as 'that handsome young man' and was approached every day by some equally handsome young Ashanti maiden who wished to be one of my many handsome wives.

Of course I had to turn them down..... for the time being anyway!

One of these wives had presented me with a handsome son, who we named Takuma. Now Takuma and I were prone to play tricks on one another. I had taught him to play these games as part of his education, and I was proud of him.

"Takuma" I would say "You must follow in your father's footsteps. Always be one step ahead of other men, for they will cheat and enslave you if they can."

So we tried to catch each other out, but of course I won most of the time.

Well about that time, I had three acres of land upon which grew maize, peppers and a few fruitful trees, and I tended them well.

Close by, the village chief had a plot of land where he used to graze his cattle.

On this particular morning I awoke to find that someone had trampled on my crops.

"You'll be sleeping alone tonight" I told my wife "I'll be on watch by our field and I'll catch this vandal without a doubt!"

So that night I crouched down in the bush, preparing for an all night vigil to catch the person causing such wanton damage.

Of course I fell asleep, but was soon rudely awakened by heavy movements nearby.

Leaping to my feet, I took hold of a large stone and cast it with all my strength towards the sound.

"Take that, you wicked man you!" but the only reply was a CRUNCH, as something heavy hit the ground.

I ran with glee to catch the intruder, but only tripped over a large cow that had obviously strayed from the Chief's field to eat my sweet maize.

"Oh! My Lord Nyame protect me. I've just killed the Chief's prize cow an' it's very very dead!"

I ran home in a panic and blurted out the story to my dear wife.

"You're a dead man" she 'comforted'. "The Chief will kill you for sure!"

"We must think up a ruse to save my skin."

So we sat up all night to come up with a trick or two.

Next day I prepared the way for our scheme, then set off to see my neighbour.

"Neighbour" I smiled "I need your help to pick ripe fruit from my trees. I'll pay you well!"

We struck up a deal and went to the field, carrying long sticks to loosen the fruits.

Pointing to a particular tree I instructed:

"You start picking, whilst I fetch the baskets!"

So he did, poking and swishing at the high branches.

Fruit began to fall, but something else fell KERPLONK. Something very large and heavy. So large it looked like a cow. In fact, it

WAS a cow. The very cow that I had killed and later hidden up in my own fruit tree. Wicked!

My neighbour began to scream:

"Lord Nyame help me! I've just killed the Chief's prize cow an' it's very very dead."

Running to the prize animal I cried in false anguish:

"Friend, good friend. What have you done? What made you kill the Chief's prize cow?"

"I was only picking your fruit when the beast fell KERPLONK at my feet. Save me Anansi!"

So I paced up and down, down and up, pretending to ponder on the matter:

"Stop your blubbering and listen to me! The Chief says that he respects honesty above all other qualities. If you go and own up before he finds you out, he's sure to be lenient. Tell him it was an accident. He won't know any different!"

"I will" said he "but before I go I must call at my yard to tell my wife where I'm going."

"Good idea," I murmured with my hand over my mouth to disguise imminent laughter "but do take the cow with you. I don't want it to be found on my land."

So he dragged the evidence away.

Well I waited for a day, then two days and a whole week passed by without any sign of a commotion from the Chief's house, so my curiosity drove me to my neighbour:

"What did the Chief say about you killing his cow?"

"Well I told him as you said, and although he was angry, he commended me for my honesty and because of that he told me to keep the cow and feed my family."

As you could imagine, I was amazed and made my way in great haste to the Chief's yard.

"Great chief! My neighbour didn't kill your cow."

The Chief seemed all confused at this remark.

Little did I know until afterwards, that my friend had never been to confess.

"Tell me about your neighbour killing my cow?" the Chief queried as he slowly sat down on his chair of office.

So I happily told him that it was myself that had slaughtered his cow and sat it up in my fruit tree.

With a mighty roar, the Chief rose and charged at me to give me such a terrible blow that I shattered into a million pieces.

As my bits fell to the floor they all became tiny spiders and the bit that was me ran off into a crack in the floor boards.

I have lived in dark nooks and crannies ever since.

I speak the truth.

* * * * * * *

Being the son of Nyame, however, did give me the ability to take on different shapes and sizes at will, but I quickly realised that retaining the form of a spider had its uses. Being so small, I was able to avoid danger by hiding in the most inaccessible places and from those lodgings I could eavesdrop on all sorts of conversations, that often proved useful in the day to day game of survival.

Sometimes I would pass amongst my people as a warrior, at other times I would be a farmer and mingle in the community, but the role of spider man was so invaluable, that this soon became my fame in the land.

What is not widely known, however, is that I was not always the beautiful shape that you see today.

When the Chief licked me with a stick, bursting me into the fragments that made me into a spider, I was just a lump, fat and round, not the slim of waist attractive spider that you love.

"I shattered into a million pieces."

How My Waist Became Slim

T his is how it happened.

Times were good for me in Ghana, as my fame was beginning to spread. The people would talk a great deal about wily fat spider man and I would waddle around the country side, being fed by all of my good friends.

My beautiful wife Aso had given me two fine sons, Takuma and Doshey and my family never lacked for anything.

But then came a particularly bad dry season and all of the crops began to fail.

My people began to suffer and although they wished to feed my family, there was scarcely enough food on their own tables and the crumbs that fell to the floor became less and less.

Gathering my family together, I said:

"If this state of affairs continues, we'll all starve to death."

Momma cried.

Takuma spoke :

"Father Anansi, what can we do?"

I thought for a moment, then declared:

"Takuma my son, you and your brother must set out on an expedition to scour the countryside to find food."

"Gladly," Takuma volunteered, "but what direction shall we take?"

"My plan was to tie a cord around my middle."

I suggested that a journey to the east might bear fruit, because I had heard from Dog that the farmer he lived with had been blessed with a good harvest the previous year.

"Father." Doshey chimed in. "Snake was telling me only yesterday that he had come across a dead cow not far from here to the west."

"Good." I responded. "You go to the west and Takuma can go to the east."

Now my plan was to tie a cord around my middle, then give one end to Takuma and the other end to Doshey.

"Both go your different ways and search for food. If you're successful, give a sharp tug on the line and we'll all come and share with you."

"Will do!" said Takuma.

"As you command." responded Doshey.

And off they went.

Well I waited. Then I waited some more. Just as I was giving up hope I felt a sharp tug on the cord from the east.

"Success! Takuma has found food at Dog's farm. Come Aso, let's see what delights are in store."

Aso took my hand and we set off to find our eldest son.

I'd just begun to sing:

> "In the east we'll find some food
> Then I can feed my little brood."

when suddenly I felt a tug to the west:

> "Clever Doshey has found the cow
> So we can fill our bellies now."

> "Which way shall we go good wife?
> East or West, that is the test!"

Another pull from Takuma was soon answered by Doshey. Then Takuma pulled again and so on, one after the other, until I felt the cord tightening around my fat belly.

"Stop it! You're hurting me!" I cried out, but to no avail.

My sons were too far away to hear and they were becoming impatient.

Harder and harder they pulled. Louder and louder I screamed, until I could scream no more, as the cord took my breath away.

Tighter and tighter, until my round, plump body was nearly cut in two.

Fortunately for me Aso saw my dilemma, and rushing into the house returned with a sharp knife and cut me free.

Too late, however, to save my roly-poly body.

Where I had been round and chubby, I now had the slimmest waist that you ever did see.

I tell no lie.

* * * * * * *

Life was good until that fateful day in the year of my Lord Nyame 1675.

I was about my chores, scampering around, looking for good places to spin a web.

Finding a good spot high up in the thatched roof of a village hut, I was spending an enjoyable afternoon swinging back and forth, weaving that intricate fly trap that my father had taught me to make. When satisfied with my handiwork, I crawled up through the reeds and rested for a while, looking down on the activities taking place in the village compound.

Evening was approaching and the fiercest heat of the sun had passed. There were thirty or so thatch-roofed huts surrounding the enclosure, all connected by wattle and daub walls, to kept the area free from marauding animals.

A mouth watering aroma drew my attention to a family who were seated around a boiling pot, enjoying their evening meal.

In the centre of the enclosure, a group of boys laughed and tormented each other, as they piled up dead wood inside a circle of stones.

To the left a woman was beating maize with a large wooden pestle and mortar and as she pounded, the regular rise and fall of the club was accompanied by an old Ashanti work song.

On the other side of the compound, a man sat cross legged before a low work table, eyes keenly focused on a goldweight figurine that he was engraving with loving care. As a boy he had been apprenticed to an Akan goldsmith and now his workmanship was the pride of the village.

An old man sat before his hut door, playing on a xylophone that he had made from wooden slats with calabashes hanging underneath, creating a delightful musical resonance that soon had me dozing, as I lay, legs outstretched on the roof.

As I dozed I had pleasant daydreams about juicy flies.

My reverie was disturbed by many voices singing.

It was dark and the village had turned out to celebrate.

What this particular assembly was all about wasn't important, because the village folks would use any excuse to gather together for a festivity.

Apparently women performers had come from the local village of Garinso and my people were singing them a song of welcome called Azaaba.

The reason for the boys' earlier effort was now evident, for a wood fire crackled and spluttered in the centre of the singing circle, throwing up sparks that lit up this happy occasion.

Making myself comfortable, I settled down for a pleasant evening of song, dance, games and story telling.

One of my favourite games was when each villager had to tell a proverb.

One by one, the young and old would rise and call out a proverb and this would go on until no more could be told.

An old man cried out:

"If you're in hiding, don't light a fire."

He was followed by a woman who declared:

"The moon moves slowly, but it still crosses the village."

Then, encouraged by his mother, a young boy garbled:

"It's a bad child that takes no advice."

And so on, until the last proverb was told.

The merrymaking continued long after midnight, but as the babbling voices began to tire, a village Elder slowly rose to his feet and clapped his hands in praise of the wonderful evening of entertainment.

He called out: "Bring the Kente cloth."

All went quiet and I sat up, all attentive, for the Kente ceremonial cloth was only brought out on special occasions. Strips of cloth, about four inches wide were woven in various rainbow colours, sizes and designs, stitched together to make a large wrap around shawl, to be worn by a chosen dignitary.

A warrior did as bid, ran to the Head man's hut, then walked back with great reverence, the shawl draped over extended arms.

A ripple of wonderment spread around the gathering, then everything became still as the Elder took the shawl and raising it in the air, he addressed the villagers and guests:

"Warriors of Navringi, wives of these brave men who protect us, the children of this blessed union and our good neighbours from Garinso, stand with me to offer thanks for our many blessings to our great and mighty Lord Nyame, God of the Sky."

With a murmur of approval everyone rose to their feet with a chant of praise and much stamping of feet.

Then he continued:

"To honour our Lord I ask Nagavoro, our revered story teller, to relate an old story." and carrying the Kente to a dignified looking Elder, he placed it gently around his shoulders.

A cheer of agreement rang through the night air and a distant lion roared its consent.

I sat up in a state of excitement, for being a story teller of some renown myself, I never missed the opportunity to add a good tale to my collection.

With a nod of assent, Nagavoro slowly rose to his feet, walked to the centre of the circle of expectant faces, loosened his neck with a shrug of his skinny shoulders, cracked his knuckles, flexed his fingers, then gave a great cough, which signalled that he was ready to begin.

The warriors squatted down and the women folk hushed their children in anticipation of the tale to come.

Nagavoro began.

'My tale will be of one who is cunning and full of tricks.'

He paused to scan the audience:

'Of one who is a villain and crafty.'

He laughed and looked to heaven:

'Of one who can be mischievous and sly.'

Before he could continue a little girl jumped to her feet, clapped her hands, did a little dance and cried out in a loud voice:

"ANANSESEM! ANANSESEM!"

Everyone laughed, but momma said:

"Shush little one! You'll spoil the story!"

Nagavoro smiled and slowly walking over to the girl, patted her on the head and said:

'Yes my child, you're quite right, for my story will indeed be about Kwaku Ananse, that rascal of a Spiderman.

Everyone whooped with pleasure.

Could I believe my ears? The story was going to be about me.

How Anansi Tricked His Father

When all had fallen silent Nagavoro began again.

'Some will say that this never really happened, but judge for yourself.'

Nagavoro was skilled at his craft, so he stood perfectly still until the restless shuffling and coughing had subsided. Arms by his side, he waited for a silent moment, then continued:

'There was a time, long long ago, when our great and mighty Sky god Nyame and his son, our beloved Anansi, lived in the heavens.

Together, they made all that there is.

Kwaku Ananse was so pleased with what he saw, that he came down to earth to live with his people, sometimes as a man, sometimes as a spider.

He listened to wonderful stories that were told by our people about anything and everything that you could imagine. Stories of green parrots, owls and mischievous monkeys.'

Nagavoro accompanied the names of each animal with the appropriate screech, hoot or gibbering dance.

'Stories of bullfrogs, hornets and creatures of all shapes and sizes and Anansi loved them all and wished to own these tales. But his father kept them in heaven for himself, only lending them out as he pleased. This didn't suit Anansi, so he constantly asked Nyame to present them to him as a gift.'

"After all I am your only son and who better than I to be guardian of these most excellent stories?"

'Nyame was not to be moved, however, replying':

"Many great story tellers wish for the tales to be their very own and hope for the fame that they will bring, so it will be better if I care for them myself."

'Anansi would not let the matter rest, however, constantly pestering and plaguing his father to give him the fables, until Nyame knew that he would have to put a stop to the annoyance somehow, so the next time he was approached by the lisping Anansi, he declared':

"I'm not prepared to give you my precious stories for nothing, but I will give you three tests and if you pass them, you may keep them for your own."

'Then Nyame slipped in a little proverb to ruffle his son, saying':

"A task from a strong man is worth two from a weak one........ like you!"

'But Anansi was not one bit ruffled. It seemed that his father didn't really know him.

Nyame thought that if he made the trials quite impossible, Anansi would fail and be so ashamed that he wouldn't dare to ask for them again. Again he didn't know his clever son.'

"Now my son, your first task will be to bring me a gourd full of wasps."

Upon hearing this the villagers clapped and whistled. They had heard this tale many times before, but they always responded with anticipation for the way that Anansi would solve this dangerous mission.

'So Anansi chuckled and went straightway to Aso, asking to borrow the gourd that she used as a water container, poured away the water and set off to find a wasp's nest that was hanging from the branch of a tree.

Sitting below he began to sing over and over again':

"What will I tell my Lord,
When he asks how many wasps will fill this Gourd?"

'It didn't take long for a curious wasp to come flying down.'

18

"What mischief are you up to Anansi?"

"No mischief! It's just that Lord Nyame has given me a riddle to solve and I don't know the answer."

'The wasp was too nosy to resist and came closer to ask':

"Tell me the riddle then!"

"My father dared me to find out how many of your family would fit into this gourd."

"Oh! the answer to that question can easily be solved," 'the wasp buzzed.' "My family will crawl in for you and you can count us as we go."

'So he buzzed up to his relatives, told them Anansi's problem, flew back and crawled into the gourd, followed by all his clan. One by one Anansi counted them in':

"One, two, three, four, five......." and so on and on, until the vessel was full and a voice cried out from inside':

"No more room, no more room, it's all full up in here!"

'With no more ado, Anansi placed a stopper over the entrance and the wasps were safely trapped.

Scuttling into the courtroom of his father, our crafty friend presented Nyame with the gourd of angry wasps, who, as you know, have been angry to this very day.

The sky god was taken aback, for he'd expected his son to fail. He showed no sign of his disappointment though, only making a resolve to beat Anansi with the second test.'

"There still remains two more, so bring me Osebo Leopard, the one some call Tiger!" 'smiled Nyame.

The courtiers gasped, for Osebo was a skilled hunter and could easily kill Anansi with one blow of his paw, but Spiderman was not perturbed, setting off straightway to find the spoor of this great cat.

Finding a trail that smelled as though it was frequently used by Osebo, Anansi dug a deep hole and covered it with branches and large leaves, then went home for his supper.

Next day he found a leopard trapped in the pit.

'One by one Anansi counted them in.'

With a touch of sarcasm in his voice Anansi called down':

"Osebo, what on earth are you doing down there?"

"Someone has set a trap for me. Please help me Anansi before they return to kill me."

"You must do me no harm if I help you."

"I swear on the name of Nyame, that I will only show you gratitude."

"Very well! Stand on your hind legs and reach up with your paws and I will reach down and pull you up."

'Osebo did as he was bid, but instead of pulling him up, Anansi took a large stick and hit him on the head.'

At this moment in the tale, Nagavoro cried "Whops!" and taking a posture as though about to leap down a hole, showed every one how Anansi jumped down and wrapped the Leopard up in web string.

'With help from his friends, Anansi carried Osebo to Nyame, who said': "You still have one more test." 'But he didn't smile this time.' "All I want you to do is to capture Python and bring him to me alive and well."

"Is that all?" laughed Anansi. 'But he wasn't laughing inside, for he knew that Onini could gobble him down with one snap of his jaws.

He really wanted Nyame's stories though, so he set out for the forest to find the enormous snake.

After two days of searching, he came upon a green tree python asleep, coiled around a branch.'

"Oh my! It must be thirty feet long."

'Anansi found a bamboo tree and taking his cutlass, cut down the longest pole, dragged it and sat with it just below Onini, singing over and over again':

> "Cane or python, python or cane,
> Is one longer or are both the same?"

Onini slowly opened one eye, flicked out his tongue and hissed': "What nonsense is this, Bredda Anansi? Are you asking to be eaten?"

"Oh no, Onini. I'm just trying to solve a riddle that my father Nyame says is impossible to unravel."

At the mention of Nyame, the python opened his other eye, for even he feared the name of the powerful Sky God.

"How can I help the son of my Lord?"

'The hypnotic voice of Onini had taken on a less threatening quality'

"Well, Nyame insists that no python has ever lived, who was longer than the longest pole of bamboo."

"Rubbish! Nothing, but nothing is as long as Onini" 'boasted the python.'

"I don't doubt it, but to prove it to my father, perhaps we could measure you beside this piece of pole that I have cut down."

"All right, I'll lay beside it and you'll see."

'Onini slithered down to the ground and lay still beside the woody stem.'

"No, no! The pole is a good two feet longer than you."

'So Onini stretched and stretched.'

Nagavoro stretched his arms into the air to make his point.

"No, no! Your tail keeps turning up, let me tie it firmly."

'Anansi took a vine and tied the python's tail to the bamboo'

"Now stretch some more."

'So Onini stretched and stretched.'

The village children joined in by stretching their arms into the air.

"No, no! Your belly keeps bending. Let me tie it firmly" 'and this Anansi did.'

"Now stretch some more and you should be taller than the pole."

'So Onini stretched and stretched.'

Everyone in the village stretched their arms high into the air.

'This was the moment.

Anansi leapt onto Onini, quickly tied a vine around his hissing head and he was caught.'

The audience whooped with delight.

'Anansi had some difficulty dragging the python, but with help from Aso, Takuma and Doshey, the angry snake was finally presented to Nyame.

"I never thought that you would succeed." 'said Nyame, but deep down he was proud of his son and willingly parted with all of his stories.

So Kwaku Ananse used bravery and cleverness to become the owner of all the wonderful folk tales of the Ashanti nation.

These stories were called Anansesem, after his name.'

Nagavoro extended both palms towards his audience and said:

'I have told a good tale and now I'll tell no more'

* * * * * *

Leaping to my many feet, I applauded this wizard of story telling, adding my voice of approval to those of the crowd gathered below.

Then the calamity overtook the village.

Suddenly from out of the enveloping darkness, there arose a dreadful commotion. Raised voices preceded a loud bang and a warrior uttered a long piercing cry and fell close by the village entrance, clutching a bleeding wound at his side. Women and children screamed and ran to their huts for shelter. The Ashanti men turned to face the intrusion and were met by a horde of shouting strangers, dressed in unfamiliar garments, who wielded clubs and broad curved swords and shot flames from long metal pipes.

The warriors were caught by surprise and without weapons, they were quickly overwhelmed and beaten into submission.

Resistance was futile.

Many a stout of spirit fighting man struggled to challenge these unwelcome marauders, but it took only a short battle to lay them low.

Humiliation quickly followed.

The British, for that was who I later discovered them to be, quickly set about the painful task of shackling the men together. Metal cuffs, riveted to the right leg of one and the left leg of another, were joined by a short chain. Then each pair of warriors were connected to other pairs by chains and metal collars, this activity accompanied by liberally applied whippings, intended to break any spirit of resistance. The task completed, it became the turn of the wailing women, who were subjected to the same fate. The children were left unfettered, as they were probably considered unlikely to leave their mothers' side and so it proved to be, for as the prisoners were led from their village, many a screaming child, unable to be carried by its mother, clung in terror to the thigh of its shuffling parent.

As the prisoners were cleared from their huts, the burning began and the unrepentant raiders put everything to the torch, looting as they went.

Smoke began to seep through the reeds of my roof, so a quick retreat was in order. Scampering down, I called for Aso, Doshey and Takuma, who soon scuttled to my side.

"What shall we do?" fretted Aso.

"I really don't know, my love, but we must try to look out for our people somehow."

"But what can we do?" pleaded Takuma.

"I really don't know yet son," I repeated "but we must follow behind, and look for an opportunity to free them."

So we did, mile after shuffling mile, day after wretched day.

Occasionally, when the winding train had to rest, I would sneak close and whisper to Nagavoro, offer comfort and talk about a possible escape, but we both knew it was futile.

Every now and then he would slip me some boiled yam, part of the meagre sustenance offered by their captors and this I shared with my family.

After great tribulation my friends arrived at the sea, to be herded into a dank fort with many other poor souls to await Nyame knows what.

By now it was being rumoured that they were being taken across the great water to be killed for food for the white men and each night the wailing of these sorry souls pulled at the core of my spirit. My cunning deserted me and I could think of no way to ease their torment.

Three days after our arrival, I was standing on the parapet of the highest wall of the fort, looking out to sea and beheld a large sailing vessel approaching from where the sun was setting on a fiery horizon.

"Look Aso! Someone's coming to rescue our people."

How wrong I was!

The wooden craft anchored just offshore and a number of small boats left the mother ship and were rowed up onto the sandy beach. The sailors stayed by the fort that night and many a young black girl was deflowered before Nyame awoke the following morning and his beaming countenance prompted the transfer of the captives, boat by boatload to the sailing ship waiting below.

Things were to worsen.

Prodded and whipped, they were driven onto the main deck, then forced below, where they suffered the ordeal of allocation to sleeping space so narrow that they were unable to lie prone, or even turn over.

Men were segregated from their women, the children left to their own devices and when the vessel was crammed full of sweating bodies, it set sail.

Aso cuddled close to me as we hid in a dark corner :

"The stench is awful down there! How will they survive?" she wept.

"I'm sorry to say sweet wife, that if this treatment continues, many of them won't arrive at their destination."

My prophesy was soon fulfilled.

After many days at sea, the conditions below were so loathsome, that fevers took hold of the passengers and many died. Without due ceremony, they were thrown overboard to the sharks.

The Ashanti people laid great store on burying their dead with dignity and showing great respect for the ancestors of the deceased, but such barbaric jailers would have none of this, treating their prisoners worse than animals.

Things became so bad below, that during the times for exercise on deck, many of the captives cast themselves overboard, rather than suffer such gross insult to their pride.

Many perished in what became called the Middle Passage, that water between the Gold Coast of Africa and Xaymaca, where the Arawaks had lived before they were wiped out by the Spaniards.

I soon began to realise that something had to be done to boost the morale of my poor people, so one night I sought out Nagavoro and whispered in his ear:

"My dear friend Nagavoro, somehow we must lift the spirits of our people to help them to survive this tribulation."

"But what can we do Anansi? Insurrection is quite impossible. Our people are too weak to fight."

"Our time to fight will come." I responded "In the meantime we must give them hope and diversion."

"I know of nothing, Bredda Anansi, that will bring back their faith."

"STORIES, my friend! The old stories that you tell so well. Let them be an inspiration. Tell the great tales of how cunning and trickery can win the day against wicked men.?

Nagavoro's eyes gleamed for a moment, then he gasped:

"Why, of course! ANANSESEM. Your exploits are just what we need to hear about."

So that night, as the ship rolled in the swell of the Caribbean Sea, Nagavoro passed a message around asking for silence. He was about to tell one of the beloved adventures of Kwaku Ananse. It was the first of many nights that tales would be told.

The crying and sobbing began to subside and the teller of stories stretched himself in his small bunk and began.

Why Anansi Lives In Plantain Trash

Once upon a time, Anansi had a most beautiful daughter and she was his pride and joy.

She was sought after by all of the eligible warriors, but Anansi wanted to keep his daughter in the bosom of his family, so he always turned her suitors away.

But one day Bredda Dryhead knocked on Anansi's door.

Now Anansi feared Dryhead, for he had the reputation of being a witch doctor and he was the only enemy that Anansi preferred to keep at arms length.

Bredda Dryhead was a dangerous adversary, so when Anansi opened the door, he was all smiles and respect for his visitor.'

"Long time no see, Bredda Dryhead. I hope you're keeping well. What can I do for you?"

'Dryhead wasn't taken in by this honey tongue and came straight to the point' :

"I hear that you have a desirable daughter, so I wish to marry."

"I'm sure that can be arranged, but first we must talk about a dowry. Maybe three cows would be fair?"

"Three cows? One barrel of dried beef is all that you'll get from me, Anansi, and if I have any trouble from you, I'll eat you up here and now."

'Anansi shook on his spindly legs.'

"Please forgive me. Your barrel will be more than enough."

"Good, bring out your daughter."

"I'm sorry, Bredda Dryhead, but my daughter is at the market and won't be home 'til late."

'Anansi lied, for his daughter was in the kitchen all the time.

So you see my people, even in the face of danger, our trickster was planning a way to escape the will of his enemy.'

"Very well." 'sneered Dryhead' "I'll bring the barrel in the morning. Have your daughter ready for me then."

'The following day Dryhead arrived at Anansi's door.'

"Here is the dowry, now bring out your daughter."

"I can't. She's gone to visit a sick aunty, but when she returns I'll send her to your house."

"Oh very well" 'snorted Dryhead, and he left.

That night Anansi's family ate beef for supper.'

A murmur accompanied the idea of 'beef for supper', for it was many a night since the prisoners had smelt the aroma of juicy meat.

'As one would expect, Dryhead was banging on Brer Anansi's door, long before the sun rose the following morning.'

"Come out you villain." 'Dryhead's voice was heard for miles around.' "You've cheated me."

"Do be calm, Bredda Dryhead" 'soothed Anansi.' "It was only an oversight on my part. You see my daughter came home so upset about her sick aunty that I forgot to tell her that you were expecting her."

"Right, I'll be taking her now."

"I'm so sorry Bredda Dryhead, but she's taken some eggs to her granny."

"Look here" 'roared Dryhead,' "If she's not at my house by morning, I'll return and eat you and all of your family, daughter and all."

'No way was Anansi going to give up his daughter, so before Dryhead came crashing through the front door that following morning, the whole family were hanging high up in the rafters.

Dryhead searched all of the rooms to no avail, until a sound attracted his attention upwards and there he saw them.

'He wriggled down in the trash.'

With a triumphant bellow, Dryhead began to stamp on the floor and crashing into the walls caused the whole building to rattle and roll, until Aso was shaken from her hold in the rafters.

Down she came and Dryhead gobbled her up.'

The children in the ship clung tightly to their mothers and whimpered.

'Takuma was the next to fall, and he was soon in the belly of Dryhead.'

The children whimpered some more.

'Then Doshey and his sister suffered the same fate.'

The children's protest was even louder.

"Right Anansi, you'll trick me no more" 'gloated the witch doctor, but before he could shake his last titbit free, Anansi, in a quiet voice said':

"Bredda Dryhead. If I fall from this height, I'll burst open and it will waste my fat and goodness, so if you would be so kind, please lay some plantain trash on the floor to break my fall, then you'll have a meal that's worthwhile."

'Dryhead paused and thought for a moment, then did as he was bid.

Anansi let go and with a scream of glee he fell onto the trash, which, of course, softened his landing.

Before his enemy could catch him, he wriggled down in the trash, and he was hidden from view.

Search as he might, Dryhead never found him.

That is why Anansi lives in trash until this very day.

My story ends.'

* * * * * * *

A spirit of hope began to permeate the cargo and suicide became less common. Exercise was demanded of the captive population, but instead of there being constant clashes between the sailors and my friends when they came on deck, there would be, with what energy could be

mustered, drumming and dancing and instead of wailing and lamenta-
tion, the songs took on a more cheerful mood.

For a time the sailors were alarmed at this change of atmosphere,
being suspicious that rebellion might be afoot, but when nothing erupted,
they were grateful to be able to relax.

Not that the brutality ended. Far from it, for many were still dying
from the fevers caused by the overcrowded conditions and even a mis-
placed glance could be rewarded with a flogging, but I was convinced
that the telling of stories was having an effect on morale.

Nagavoro also noticed the apparent benefit of storytelling in passing away the miserable hours, and soon his stories were joined by the
proverb game.

Just as well, for there were many tribulations to come.

Little did they know that soon they were to face a worse indignity
on an auction block.

We arrived in Jamaica.

The freight was whipped up to the deck, driven down the gang-
plank, shuffling and flinching to the docks below, where they were herded
into cattle pens to await the arrival of plantation owners.

It was midday, and the sun beat down mercilessly on the cooped up
captives. The only sanitation was an insufficient number of soon filled
buckets placed inside the enclosure, but one civilized concession at least
was permitted, for families were allowed to reunite with great joy, as
men hugged their wives and children after their long separation.

Two days and nights passed and a few rebellious incidents within
the pens were quickly put down with well placed musket butt and bull
whip, but on day three there was great activity, each victim being brought
out, stripped naked and made to spruce up by washing from head to
toe.

Some important event was afoot.

At eleven o'clock in the forenoon, a fat ruddy faced official, carrying a long staff of office walked down the dock, swinging and ringing a

large brass hand bell. Approaching a raised platform, he struggled up the wooden steps, banged his staff and bellowed out:

"OYEZ! OYEZ! OYEZ!" then putting down bell and staff, he leisurely unrolled a scroll of parchment and when satisfied that enough people had gathered round, he spoke out in a voice that rang across the dock :

"Let it be known in this year of our Lord 1676, that on this fourth day of June, there be for auction, two hundred and twenty four negroes, who have survived the journey on the recently docked ship Seagull.

These will be sold as slaves, to be worked at the discretion of their owners."

He paused for a moment to wipe the trickling sweat from his blotchy face, then replacing his 'kerchief back in his coat sleeve, he continued:

"Please be aware that they are not yet broken and will be in need of the strictest discipline.

The ship's captain reports that this assignment have not shown serious signs of rebellion, but many are from the Ashanti tribe and may need firm handling.

Feel free to examine the goods, but you are advised not to place your fingers in a mouth whilst examining the teeth."

Many of the gathering laughed, understanding well this particular hazard.

The auctioneer introduced the first lot:

"Here is a healthy family, comprising a sturdy ox of a man, his woman and their infant son." Turning to a stockman he waved:

"Bring 'em up!" and a crack of the whip encouraged the dejected trio to mount the 'block' to be viewed and examined by potential buyers from amongst the ogling crowd.

The muscles of the man were felt and admired.

The auctioneer noticed the particular attention shown to the woman by a male customer whose examination was more than thorough.

"Yes, sir! She'll be a useful asset to keep around the house."

Some women sniggered, but others tutted to express their disapproval.

"Who'll start the bidding at one hundred guineas for the three?"

There was no response.

"Come now, I can't start the bidding for less than eighty. The man is going to be a workhorse, the woman will have many uses and the infant will make a good worker if he grows up anything like his father."

Raising a silver topped cane, a plantation owner standing at the back proffered :

"I'll offer you twenty five guineas for the man."

So the bidding commenced and the man was sold, to be led away, protesting in vain.

His woman was sold to the molesting merchant. Separated from her man, she had to be physically carried away, shrieking and fighting. The boy was thrown in as a bonus.

The previous excitement of being reunited was shattered.

Aso and myself watched the sickening procedure go on until the sun set and the cattle pens were empty.

As the plantation owners left with their wretched slaves, I encouraged my family to climb aboard one of their carriages. Traveling through the night, we left the chained and walking Ashanti to catch up with us the following day.

Finding a safe lodging beside the driver, we settled for what turned out to be an all night journey. To while away the time, I told a story to Aso and the boys to make them laugh and take their minds from the harrowing scenes of the day.

How I Was Tricked By Bredda Monkey

O ne day, not long after I came down from the sky, I had been toiling hard in my yam field and was starting to feel hungry. "What do I fancy to eat?" I said to myself.. "Some corn might be nice, or perhaps some of my own yam. Better still, what about a nice juicy steak of monkey meat. Yes! Just what my belly is calling for."

So I went home, heaved the stove onto my back and staggered to Monkey Island.

Putting it down in a suitable place, I climbed into the oven and began to shout:

"Tishiki, Tishiki," (or "tickle me, tickle me.") then jumping out I danced around, making considerable noise, until I came to the attention of a band of monkeys.

"What are you doing Bredda Anansi?" howled the monkeys.

"I'm playing a game called Tishiki, Tishiki."

"And how do you play this game?" clamoured the monkeys.

"Easy" I laughed. "We just put sticks under this oven, light them up, I get inside, you shut the door and when it gets too hot I shout out:

'Tishiki. Tishiki'. Then you let me out. Easy!"

"Can we play? Can we play?" hollered the monkeys.

"Of course you can, but it's my turn first" I teased.

"All right. All right" and when the fire crackled I popped into the oven.

"Tishiki, Tishiki."

I was in but a moment, then I called out "Tishiki, Tishiki."

The monkeys laughed and let me out.

"What a good game" they cried, jumping up and down with glee. "Our turn now! Our turn now!"

I opened the oven door for them, they all piled in and I shut the door down tight.

They were in only a few moments, when I heard them all cry:

"Tishiki, Tishiki."

I sat in the shade of a banana tree.

"Tishiki, TISHIKI!" the monkeys cried with more urgency.

I crossed my eight legs.

"TISHIKI, TISHIKI!" The monkeys wailed.

I dozed in the shade until the monkeys were well baked, then I had me a great feast and slept until late in the afternoon.

As the sun set, I packed up my stove and made my way home.

I hadn't noticed a monkey watching me from a banana tree.

A week later, I was leaving my house to tend the yam field, and found a group of monkeys gibbering around my stove.

"What happens?"

"We've come to play Tishiki."

"Good!" I said out loud.

But to myself I said: "Lovely, I'll get a free breakfast before I go to work."

I lit the oven wood, then invited the monkeys to climb in.

"Your turn first, Bredda Anansi, your turn. We don't know how to do it."

So without thinking I popped into the stove.

The monkeys yelled for joy, leapt forward and slammed the door.

"Tishiki, Tishiki."

The monkeys tittered.

"Tishiki, TISHIKI."

The monkeys danced.

"TISHIKI, TISHIKI."

Then the monkeys played until I was well cooked, then sat together to feast on juicy spider meat.

So now I keep well away from Monkey Island.

I'm going to say no more.

* * * * * * *

I chuckled to myself.

I always enjoyed telling this story against myself, so I looked to my family for approval, but found them all to be fast asleep.

What else could I do but snuggle against Aso and join them.

Early in the morning we arrived at the sugar cane plantation.

The owner's house was set high up on the slope of a hill, overlooking the pristine turquoise waters of the Caribbean Sea, that merged with a clear blue sky to cool the fiery rising sun.

What a beautiful house it was.

A flight of stone steps curved up to an open terrace, leading to the impressive entrance of a fine double storey dwelling. Everything was spacious and well able to accommodate and entertain numerous guests. I scurried around, taking in the superb furnishings and lavish drapes, that indicated that the family who lived here had certainly made their way in the world and become rich.

It wasn't until I rambled around the fields on the following day, that I discovered that the pathway to this opulent life lay over the bodies of a multitude of branded slaves, whose lot was horrendous.

Cattle received better treatment than did these poor souls, who were considered by some to be a species given by their God, to be beasts of burden for the white man.

Aso, myself and our sons, lived here and there on the plantation for some thirty years.

During this time, all of our companions that had sailed on the vile ship Seagull were worked to death.

Few slaves survived ten years of such hard labour.

Some, however, escaped.

During my regular visits with my friends, I heard and joined in the telling of folk tales and soon there were added to the good old time stories of Africa, a number of tales about a paradise of freedom here in Jamaica.

Somewhere, in a rugged mountainous district, there lived a people who called themselves the Maroons, the 'fierce and unruly' ones. They were descendants of ex-slaves, who had escaped their masters after the British took the island from the Spanish in 1655, and they had made their home in nearly impenetrable terrain, to make a stand against slavery.

Some say that they had muskets, given to them by the Spaniards and that they were fighting and resisting the British soldiers under the leadership of a warrior named Cudjoe.

Slave rebellion was not uncommon in Jamaica after 1678 and these were always ruthlessly put down by the authorities, but the British were unable to subdue Cudjoe, Nanny and the runaway slaves of Nanny Town.

They said that Cudjoe was the only man who could cut off the head of a large bull with a single slash of his pocket knife and with a reputation like that, it's no wonder that it became the ambition of many a slave to join him, so in 1726, I set out with my family to find this land of liberty.

Heading into the highlands of Blue Mountain country, we searched for many weeks to find their hideaway .

We were eventually drawn to this refuge by the sound of drumming and the blowing of Abeng horns.

I told Aso and the boys to stay in hiding whilst I checked how safe it would be to visit.

Peeping from the bush, I watched the dancing and singing of men, women and children, who swayed and stamped around a wood fire.

For a moment, my mind was carried back to that fateful day when our slavery began in Ghana.

Then I saw her sitting outside her hut.

From descriptions gleaned from plantation slaves on our journey, it was that elusive Grandy Nanny, the Queen of the Maroons. She was a strong featured woman, with the most piercing eyes, and although small and lean, she had the bearing of a fearless Ashanti warrior.

Many claimed that she was an Obeah woman, endowed with old witchcraft knowledge from the old country, so with bad memories of Dryhead, it was with trepidation that I stepped out into the open and approached her throne.

All fell silent and spears guarded my approach.

Nanny arose to her feet, turned to face me and with outstretched arms, she greeted me:

"My good friend Kwaku Ananse! You are welcome here!"

For one moment I was unable to move or respond.

"Thank you Excellency. You know me then?"

"My dear Anansi, I've known of you since I was a child sitting on my mother's knee, when she told me tales of your exploits. For days now, my spies have been reporting on your journey to find us."

Waving to a sentry on the edge of the clearing she commanded: "Tell Aso, Takuma and Doshey to join us!"

So we sat together enjoying food and hospitality, whilst this leader of her people told me her story.

"Well Anansi, we have friends living with us who escaped the bukra massa. They remember the comfort you gave to them on the slave ship Seagull and we all thank you.

We've been fighting guerrilla warfare here in the mountains for six years now, with great success.

We're keeping the old religion alive and we would all sooner die than relinquish our freedom to those brutal white men. We're outgunned and outnumbered, but my people are so courageous and with the help of Obeah magic, we'll never be beaten."

After Nanny had told many an exciting story of skirmishes and victories, she turned to me and said :

"Right Anansi, that's enough of myself and the maroons. It's time for ANANSESEM. I'm sure the gathering would love to hear one of YOUR adventures."

She scanned the motley circle of villagers for some response and was greeted by a hearty rumble of approval.

All fell silent and Aso nodded, but needing no encouragement, I cleared my throat to begin:

Why Tumble Bug Rolls In the Dung

I'll tell you a story and this is how it began.

Long ago, Bredda Bug and I were good friends and we spent much of our time wandering around the countryside together.

One day we were met by Bredda Elephant.

"Have you two heard the news?" he enquired. "The King is offering the hand of his daughter in marriage to anyone who can bring him a pottery jar full of gold coins!"

Well, I was all ears, because I'd heard that the King's daughter was quite a beauty.

Unfortunately I was short of money at the time.

"I've seen the Princess and I would be glad to marry her" said Bug. "I'll go home and get my money jar!"

"Wait for me, I'll go with you to the palace" said I, and I scuttled off to find a jar. Filling it with cow dung, I hid it about my person, then hurried off to meet Bredda Bug, who by now was heading towards the Palace with his jar of gold coins.

As we walked and talked together we passed a shop.

"I'm very thirsty. Let's stop for a cool drink."

"Good idea." agreed Bug.

'He scattered the contents...'

We went inside, placed our jars on the counter, ordered some lemonade and sat to talk for a while with the shopkeeper.

"Well friend, we must be on our way to the Palace."

So picking up a jar, I set off.

What bug hadn't noticed, however, was that I'd picked up his jar of money and he had pocketed the jar of cow dung.

My trick was working.

Not far up the road we came to the King's Palace and stating our business to the palace guards we were allowed to approach his royal Highness.

Before Bug could say a word, I addressed the King.

"Oh, Mighty King. I believe that you are offering the hand of your daughter in marriage to whosoever can bring you a pot of gold."

"Indeed I am." nodded the King.

"Then behold!" I said and emptied the jar, scattering gold coins all over the King's expensive carpet.

"Waaaah" I played to my audience for proper dramatic effect.

"Hold on a minute" cried out Bug. "I've got a jar of money too!"

Taking out his jar, he scattered the contents over the priceless carpet.

My dear, there was such a commotion in the Palace that you wouldn't believe.

The King screamed:

"You nasty fellow! How dare you come into my Palace and throw dung all over my beautiful carpet. Clean up your mess this very minute. Take it out of my yard or I'll have you flogged!"

So poor Bug had to collect up all of the dung, roll it up, and heaving and tumbling, push the ball of filth off the carpet, down the Palace steps and into the yard.

Sometimes he's called Dung Beetle, but we know him better as Tumble Bug, and he's been tumbling in filth to this very day.

What happened to me? I married the King's daughter, didn't I!
Yes! Anansi did it.

* * * * * * *

The following day Nanny and I walked alone to talk warrior talk.

We chatted about the military tactics that she used so effectively against the British troops. It seemed that the wily way of exploiting the mountainous terrain was her main strength, but an Obeah trick or two were part of her arsenal, like the stories that were told of how she would turn her back on the soldiers, raise her skirts and mock and challenge them to fire at her. Volley after volley of musket fire had no effect and to the great consternation of her enemies, she would run away laughing. Some cynics suggested that she wore a skirt of iron, but I'm sure that magic was her protector.

I gave her advice though, about confounding the British by using 'bush' camouflage to conceal her warriors. Later I named this covering 'Cakoon.'

I was happy to join in during the ambushes that were set to trap the uninvited predators.

One time, dressed in 'war bush,' we spread ourselves around an area of wooded land near the exit from a ravine, that was soon to be reconnoitered by the British. Nanny's spies, were, as usual, accurate with their information and before long we heard the crunching of stones under many clumsy feet, announcing the arrival of a company of the British military. Silence and surprise were our weapons, so we stood perfectly still, merging into the green surroundings as the troops fanned out with bayonets fixed, looking for our guerrilla band. We held our breath, so that no telltale quiver of cakoon would announce our presence.

Suddenly, an Abeng horn sounded and 'bushes' exploded into life. Screaming warriors descended on the soldiers, firing muskets, thrusting and slashing with spear and cutlass, catching the invaders totally unprepared for the onslaught.

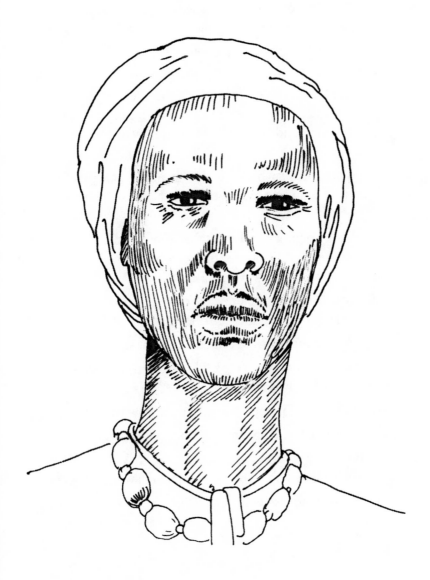

Nanny of the Maroons

Unable to form ranks against this attack, the soldiers fled in total disarray, to report yet again that Nanny had bested them.

My family and I settled in Nanny Town and shared the tribulations and joy of this brave people for some five years, but then I became restless and felt the need to move on.

On the night before we left to return to the valley, Nanny gave a farewell party and during the festivities, she turned to Aso and said:

"My dear Crooky!" (for that's what she affectionately called my wife) "We're all going to miss you all and we'll carry sweet memories of your stay. It would be nice if you could say a few words of farewell."

Crooky (for that's what we called her after that night) rose to her feet, bowed to Nanny and addressed the gathering in that quiet voice of hers:

"We thank you for your hospitality and we hope that you won't forget us. I know that it would be my husband's wish that you keep our memory alive by telling stories of our exploits.

My husband is incorrigible and full of lovable tricks, so as a farewell gift may I tell you a tale of trouble in the Anansi household.

Applause sprang from the gathered Maroons.

Crooky liked to sit when she told stories, so taking a place beside her good friend Nanny, she began:

'This tale of mine is not aimed at anyone in particular.....'

Everyone laughed at her knowing look at Anansi......

..... 'but a certain person that I know well, is like Leopard, who lets rain beat on his skin, for he knows that it cannot wash away his spots.'

There was another snicker of laughter.

Anansi's Grave

"Well, this particular day I was gathering some peas from our small piece of land. I was working hard as usual, unlike Anansi, who was in his favourite place, swinging in a web string hammock that he had spun high up, under the verandah.' "Good wife," he crooned "cook me up some of those delicious looking peas for my lunch."

"Only if you come help me gather them!" I replied.

Anansi then used the ploy that was his usual trick to avoid work and with a low moan, he said in a weakening voice':

"Dear wife, I've suddenly taken ill! I couldn't possibly do any work in the garden!"

'Knowing all of his tricks, however, I quickly replied':

"What a pity! You won't be able to enjoy my lovely pea soup. Perhaps when you're feeling better, you'll be able to help me."

'But my Anansi was too stubborn to climb down and played his 'sick' game for three more days. Yes! he would prefer to go hungry, than be beaten at his own game, but on the fourth day he changed his tactics by calling his family around him to bid them a last farewell':

"I'm about to die, so here is my last wish. Please bury me in a wooden coffin in the middle of mother's plot of peas. Then drill a hole in the lid and make a tunnel in the soil to the surface, so that my duppy may come up to guard the peas for you every night."

'So we played along with his little game.

He pretended to be dead so we buried him, carried out his wishes to the letter, then prepared for 'nine nights'.

'...Anansi came up for his usual feast...'

Takuma, Doshey and I hid in a spot close by the garden and soon after sunset our vigil was rewarded.

Who did we see, climbing up through the hole in the coffin, but Anansi himself. He looked around furtively, then crept into the kitchen to fetch a cook pot of water. Collecting some kindling, he soon had a fire burning and picking some peas, it was not long before pea soup was bubbling happily on the flames.'

"Well you scoundrel"

'I choked and was on the verge of running out to confront my scheming husband, when Takuma held me back and whispered':

"Patience mother. We'll teacher him a lesson that he won't forget."

'So I pretended not to mind that my plump peas were being stolen and watched as my clever son planned for our revenge. .

The following day Takuma took two stakes and nailed them together to resemble a cross, drove it into the ground near his father's grave, put an old hat on top, then painted it all over with sticky tar.

We all took up our sentry duty at sundown.

We watched and then we watched some more, until at last Anansi came up for his usual feast of pea soup. Noticing the tar doll, he approached with a greeting:'

"Good evening, Sir!"

'No reply, so once again he greeted the silent visitor:'

"I said good evening, Sir!"

'Still no response.'

"Have you no respect, Sir? Good evening I said!"

'Silence.'

"I've a mind to thump you for such bad manners."

'Of course, our stump was saying nothing, so Anansi gave it a great blow on the head.'

"Bap." Crooky punched her hand with her fist.

'The tarred stump held onto Anansi's hand and it was stuck tight.'

"Let me go man or I'll give you another smack!"

'We know that there was no reply, so "Bap," my husband gave it a mighty pound with his other hand, which became stuck as well.

Doshey, Takuma and I almost spoiled the sport by nearly laughing out loud.'

"Let me go! Let me go, before I get really mad," 'screamed my husband, and he let fly with a mighty kick, which stuck on impact.

One last kick with the remaining leg had Anansi well and truly fixed and he howled and howled with rage, until my voice silenced him.'

"Well, well, my pretty man. You've played one trick too many this time. If only I could believe that it would teach you a lesson."

'The boys and I came out of hiding laughing our sides sore. We retired to bed, leaving father to stay all night, hanging from the stump, giving him plenty of time to ponder on his fate.

It rained heavily much of the night and Anansi was a sorry sight when we released him next morning.

He was so ashamed that he climbed up into the rafters and there you will find him to this very day.

I'm sure that Anansi wishes that I hadn't told you this tale.'

But I laughed at such a good story told so well.

* * * * * * *

We said our farewell to the Maroons the following morning, and set off, like wandering nomads, to continue our journey of exploration in this land of wood and water.

During years of roaming, we were kept up to date with the goings on by listening to the 'bush telegraph.'

Three years after our departure, Nanny Town fell to the British, but we were pleased to hear that she regained her home later.

Nanny was angry when she heard that the Maroon General Cudjoe had made a treaty with the British. Her distrust of the British was well founded, for the invaders continually broke their side of any bargain.

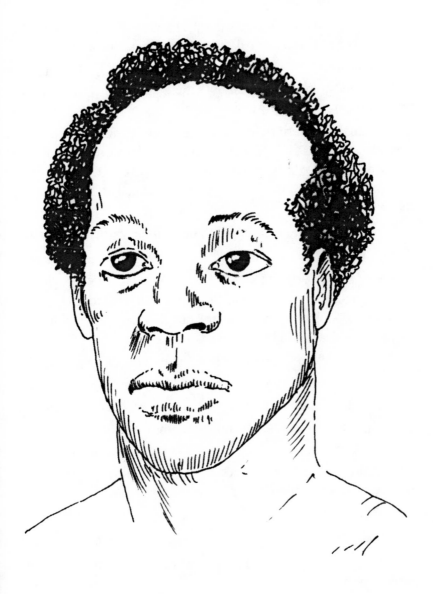

Sam Sharpe

The brave Maroon struggle for freedom has never been suppressed, even up to the present day.

Over the next one hundred years the island saw many armed slave revolts, all of which were put down in a most brutal manner.

During these bad times, my family and I relied on poor slave families for refuge and in spite of the pain and suffering around us, many a pleasant evening was passed by trading a story or two.

Eventually, we arrived in Montego Bay during 1832, to be told that we had just missed a rebellion, later to be called the Christmas Rebellion, which had also been ended with terrible retribution and bloodshed and that its leader Sam Sharpe was to be hanged at the Parade the following day.

Curious to meet Sam, I slipped through his prison cell window that night.

"Good evening, Massa Sharpe. How goes it with you?"

Maasa Sharpe was sitting on the bare wooden boards of his bunk, reading the book of his religion, the one they called the Bible. He looked up with a startled expression:

"Well, well! I never thought I would meet Brother Anansi before joining my saviour."

Sam was a follower of a god they called the Christ.

"What brings you here?" continued Sam.

"I'm really not sure," I pondered "but my mission in life seems to revolve around the idea of freedom, so I was hoping to find out what has driven you to lay down your life in this way."

"That's a long story my friend."

"Well, I've no pressing business. I'd love to hear it."

"Very well, but I'll keep it short." said Sam, as he leaned back against the rough plastered wall:

"I was born as a slave in Montego Bay in 1801 and suffered the usual indignities of my position, but even as a boy I believed that there must be a time when slavery must end."

He was silent for a moment, probably preoccupied with memories of his childhood.

"I applied myself to learn how to read and write and whenever I could, I would get hold of discarded white men's newspapers and follow the work and activities of a group of people in England, who wished to abolish the slave trade.

My local Baptist Church was sympathetic to this crusade, so I became a member of the local chapel and because of my self education, was soon acclaimed as a preacher.

Coming to realize that the teachings of the bible didn't condone the state of the black slaves of Jamaica, I often made such comment in my sermons.

But I also recognized that the Bible tells us not to be violent, so I taught my congregation that the pathway to liberation was by the peaceful withdrawal of their labour."

"A good trick, Reverend."

I was to encounter this method of political action later in my travels.

"Well, it would have been, Brother Anansi, if only my people had remembered my teachings about restraining themselves from physical violence.

Anyway, I knew that to withhold the slave work force at just the right time, would cause havoc at harvest time, so we spread the word around the district that on Christmas Day we would all 'down tools,' and use 'passive resistance' to force the plantation owners to reconsider their not paying for our work.

This was the right time and year, because the Abolitionists were winning their case in the English Parliament.

Then hot heads spoiled my whole plan.

They put the Kensington Estate in St. James to the torch, bringing down retribution on us all. A rampage of burning followed until the militia responded with terrible ferocity.

The hard hand of British justice has executed many hundreds of my comrades and I myself await to meet my Jesus, when they hang me on the gallows in the Market Place tomorrow."

"Lord Nyame preserve you. How can I be of comfort?"

"Anansi, my friend! All I would ask is that you sit with me through these dark hours until daylight and a good story to make me smile wouldn't go amiss."

Cowitch
And Mr. Foolman

I remember a time when Mr Foolman fooled me.

There is a very unpleasant poisonous plant in Jamaica called Cowitch.

Whether it makes cows itch, I don't know, but it certainly would make me itch if I were scratched by it.

A gentleman who lived near me had a field that was overrun by the horrible stuff and he wanted it clearing.

Nobody wanted the job of course, because they would all end up itching and scratching and go home in a terrible state.

So the gentleman tried a crafty ruse.

"If anyone can get rid of my cowitch without scratching themselves, they can have the pick of the best cow from my herd."

Well everyone who tried, failed.

So I called over to him one day:

"I'll cut down your cowitch without scratching."

The man didn't believe that I could clear his land without itching and scratching myself, so he sent one of his workman to ensure that I didn't break his rules.

Well, I started on the job with my cutlass, but it wasn't long before the cowitch made me itch and itch and itch.

I called to the workman, who was watching me like a John Crow bird and started up a conversation:

'I pointed to my side...'

"The cow that I want from your employer is black on his side somewhere about here."

I pointed to my side and gave it a little scratch without him noticing.

"And down this side he has a white patch about here."

I pointed to the other side and gave it a secret scratch as well.

"Its red about here."

Another point and a scratch.

"It has patches like shoes on its feet."

So I scratched my feet and he wasn't any wiser.

I carried on like this until I'd cut down all of the cowitch bush, but the gentleman wasn't too pleased when I claimed my cow, even though he couldn't deny the evidence of his workman who had said:

"I never once saw Anansi scratch himself."

I needed some help to butcher my new cow, so I looked for someone gullible to help.

Mr Foolman was passing by at that very moment and I thought:

"This is the very fool that I'm looking for."

(But Mr Foolman was not as foolish as I thought him to be.)

"Let's find a quiet place, where we can butcher the cow in peace, then you can take some home for your family."

Mr Foolman took me to a secluded place, but I didn't realize that it was close to his yard.

"We must make a fire to roast the beef." but Mr Foolman pleaded that he didn't know where he could get fire.

"Over there! Over there!" I said impatiently, and pointed to a wisp of smoke that rose lazily into the air in the distance.

"Oh! That's too far away."

I became vexed and walked off grumbling that if I wanted the job doing, I'd have to do the job myself."

Whilst I was away Mr Foolman set out to cheat me.

(I was told later what had happened in my absence, by my old friend Mister Owl, who had a ringside seat in a Cotton Wood tree nearby).

As soon as I left, Mr Foolman called his family, butchered the cow, cut it up and carried the portions off to his yard. All that they left behind was its tail.

To trick me, Mr Foolman dug a hole, planted the tail as deep as he could, stamped around it to make it firm, just leaving the tuft showing above the ground.

As I returned, Mr Foolman was hanging on to the tail crying out:

"Brer Nancy! Brer Nancy! The whole cow's gone under the ground and only left his tail sticking out. Help me! Help me!"

I ran up, took hold of the tail and we pulled.........

.........and we PULLED.........

............and we P U U U U LLED.

Suddenly the tail broke off in our hands, so that's all of my cow we had left to share.

So with all of my cunning, I didn't even have enough tail for ox-tail soup and I never did find my cow.

My story ends.

* * * * * * *

'Daddy' Sharpe and I sat all through the night exchanging stories, mine about myself, his about his god Jesus.

His stories were intriguing, his Saviour being a man after my own heart, for Jesus also wanted to 'free' his people.

I was amazed, for in spite of his forthcoming execution, Sam was so calm, and to this very day I can remember his last comment as martial

Paul Bogle

steps reverberated outside his cell, heralding his last walk to the gallows:

"Don't fret about me Anansi" he smiled "I'd rather die upon yonder gallows than live in slavery."

Within two years of his death slavery was abolished.

Unfortunately, this didn't change the lot of the Afro-Jamaican population.

We heard the singing and dancing in the streets to celebrate the first hint of freedom, but the plantation owners just smiled, for no way were they going to relinquish their hold on my black friends.

Crooky and I decided to take the boys to find our old friends the Maroons in St. Thomas, but things had changed.

Nanny was dead and various treaties had been signed with the British, which were conditional on them not sheltering runaway slaves. The Maroons had become solitary and less the symbol of freedom for their comrades in arms throughout the island. The old fervor for liberty was dying. To their shame the British were buying them out.

Eventually, some thirty years later, we found ourselves living in a place called Stony Gut.

There were signs of the free village life returning and the people began to meet together in the way I remembered, back home in Ghana.

My family were made welcome, free to wander about, taking up residence in any old nook and cranny that took our fancy.

Keeping our ears open for local gossip, we were soon able to piece together the current state of affairs and how life had changed since the abolition of slavery was pronounced.

One sultry night I was sitting amongst a gathering of the villagers and they all freely expressed their feelings to me.

One village elder told me:

"We had expected so much from our new found freedom, but its dawned on us that the British, who no longer have the whip and shackle to contain us, are now using the legal system to keep us down."

"Yes," continued another, "we've all been compelled to serve a four year apprenticeship, then we're still dependent for work on our previous bosses, who only want us to toil long hours for a meagre wage."

"Aye!" responded another angry villager. "If we start up on our own, they charge us rent for everything. Land, houses and even on the burial plots for our family. We're forced to leave the plantations and take to land on higher ground, which is less fertile and most rocky to farm. All of the best land has been spoken for by the plantation owners."

A woman intervened:

"Not only rent, though. We're forced to pay taxes. Taxes on roads, toll taxes and taxes on food. Even our canoes and donkeys are taxed, but the British governors make no effort to improve our living conditions, accusing us of being lazy and not worth their effort."

"Indeed," responded the first elder "They try to undermine us, by bringing in paid Indian workers. In fact, the authorities have used every trick at their disposal to keep us down."

Whilst we talked, a serious looking man, dressed in a dark suit and sporting a silver chain that dangled from waistcoat button to pocket, slipped quietly into our midst and sat down.

He was a man whose name I was to put alongside those heroes I most admire.

A villager turned to me and said:

"Brer Anansi, may I introduce you to our spiritual leader Mister Paul Bogle?"

"Pleased to meet you, sir!"

"Well, well, if it isn't Bredda Anansi. I've been hearing all about your exploits. My reason for visiting the village was to talk about the problems that a certain magistrate is causing us, but I'm sure that can wait until we've heard a good story."

The first Elder called out:

"Somebody fetch Granny Clarice."

Clarice was the oldest woman in the village and she had a gift for storytelling.

A group of children found their senior citizen on the porch overlooking her yard, rocking her ancient wrinkled body on a favoured seat, and with great respect they escorted her to the assembly, one holding her arm, others carrying her chair.

Brother Bogle begged her to tell a story in my honour.

Sitting on her rocking chair and giving me a nod of recognition, she began:

When Anansi's Wife Tried To Leave Him

'**D**o you remember a time when Kwaku Ananse lived amongst the Ashanti people of Ghana?

His king had three daughters, the names of whom he kept a secret from his people.

He had named his youngest daughter Uso Ya, his middle daughter Eso Ya and his eldest daughter Aso Ya.

About this time it was the custom for eligible young warriors to compete to win the hand of one of these maidens, but the king would only give up a princess for marriage if they were able to guess the name of each and every daughter.

Many a worthy young man would stand before the court and offer up names for the daughters, but not one succeeded.

One warrior suggested':

"Asuni, Mosani and Samoni."

'The king laughed.

Another suitor proposed':

"Shana, Romana and Boswana."

'The queen giggled.

So the guessing went on for days on end and many an admirer was turned away from the palace.

Well! Bredda Anansi heard about the king's offer and decided to try his hand, not by guessing, but by fooling everyone with his cunning.

'...sing him to sleep with a

Searching through the nooks and crannies under the living quarters of the three daughters, Anansi eventually found himself lying quiet and still right beneath the bedroom of Aso Ya. It had been a long day listening to all of the contestants trying to guess names, so she was resting on her bed.

Anansi heard the door open and listened as the queen said':

"Well Aso Ya, it seems that another day has passed and no-one has guessed your name or those of your sisters Eso and Uso."

'That's all Anansi needed to hear, so scuttling away, he went home to sleep. Rising early, he washed and smartened himself up, to present himself at court to 'guess' the three names, in competition with many other hopefuls.

The first man said':

"Defuli, Feludi and Leleeli."

'The king guffawed.

Another advanced and declared':

"Shaydosh, Dashyosh and Hasylosh."

'The queen chuckled as the names became sillier and sillier.

Anansi waited until the last guess had been made, then stepped out from the gathered crowd, took up a scholarly stance and declared:'

"My king, one of your daughters is named Uso Ya, another Eso Ya and the third is Aso Ya."

'The king and queen were astounded and never guessed his trick, so a splendid wedding took place. Anansi married the eldest daughter and took her home to his yard, where they lived happily with their soon to come son Takuma.'

Wagging her finger at the gathered villagers, Clarice tutted her teeth and observed:

'All would have been well with the Spider man and his family if it hadn't been for his boastful nature.'

She turned to me, and with an apology, explained:

'Well that's what the man who told me this story said.'

The whole village burst into laughter.

Clarice continued:

'Anansi was well known for his fiddle playing and singing songs and one day Aso asked him to put Takuma to bed and sing him to sleep with a lullaby. So he did.'

"Hush, little Spider man and listen if you can. I'll tell you how I tricked the king of this land."

'So Anansi bragged in his lullaby, about the underhanded way that he had won Aso's hand in marriage. Little did he know that she was listening all the time.

Well you can imagine her anger as she packed her bags and headed for the palace.

Anansi heard her slam the gate and ran after her.'

"Where are you going in such a huff?"

"I heard your lullaby, so I'm going home to mother."

"It wasn't me singing dear wife. It was the wood cutter."

"You lie!" 'she replied and continued on her way.

Anansi took a shortcut through the bush and hid beside the pathway where Aso would pass, and as she approached he changed his voice and began to sing the song about his cunning.

Aso stopped to listen and thinking it was the wood man, she spun around and hurried back home.'

"So you come back woman?"

'Anansi had taken the short route and was waiting for her.'

"I'm sorry, dear husband, for doubting your word. It was indeed the wood cutter who made up that wicked song."

'Aso made a fuss over her man for weeks to come.

Anansi just smiled, but Jack Mandora at heaven's gate was not in favour of his wicked ways.'

* * * * * * *

As I looked around the village people, I just grinned.

George William Gordon

A wave of applause flowed and Clarice sat back on her rocking chair, lit her chalk pipe and sighed.

"Well told, Clarice." commended Paul.

Clarice merely closed her eyes and nodded.

I turned to Mister Bogle:

"What were you going to say about trouble with a magistrate?"

"Oh Yes! Anansi. For some time now the authorities have been taking a hard line with our village. Taxing us for this and for that and increasing our land rents until life has become most difficult. Some of the planters have tried to evict their small holding tenants, but have been unsuccessful, so now they're getting the local magistrates to use legal process against them. One of our brethren appears in court tomorrow in Morant Bay, so we have sworn to support him."

"May I join you?"

"Of course you may Bredda Anansi. Any help will be welcome."

So it was on the following day, the 7th of October 1865, that Bogle, myself and a large gathering of farmers marched to Morant Bay to make due protest. I led the procession, playing my fiddle and singing with the horn blowers, little knowing the bloody sequence of events that was to be unleashed.

When we arrived, an endeavour was made to rescue the villager who was before the Magistrate for refusing to pay his rent, but a scuffle broke out and some of the policemen were injured in the melee.

"You'll pay for this!" the magistrate shouted as we left, so we knew that more trouble was on the way and two days later a body of police officers arrived at Stony Gut with orders to arrest my friend Paul and others accused of causing the disturbance.

We were ready for them, however, and it was they who found themselves wearing the handcuffs.

Next day we returned to the bay, to make it most clear that we were expecting justice.

Serious fighting broke out and we were at 'war'.

Marcus Garvey

Chanting "Cleave to the black!" we successfully took over a large area of St.Thomas Parish, but not long after, we had to face the might of the British Empire. A gunboat rushed soldiers to the scene and the Maroons were bribed with bounties to capture our leader.

To their shame they did.

My dear friend Nanny must have moaned in her grave, to see black turning upon black in this way.

Burning, execution and flogging followed and Paul and his good friend George William Gordon, who as a parliamentary candidate had represented the cause in Government House, were jointly accused of instigating the rebellion and hanged.

Both of them, alongside Nanny and Sharpe, were to become heroes of the nation.

I escaped!

Crooky and I grieved for our friends and our sadness deepened, as we shared our feelings about the continuing poor state of our people.

"They've been in slavery for nearly two hundred years and although its been abolished, the conditions for the people are still not improving. When will they see the fruits of freedom?"

"Never mind, my love." comforted Crooky "We'll give them hope with Anansesem."

We did so for many more years, travelling around the countryside, telling tales as we went.

During our wanderings, a terrible war took place between Britain, her allies and a nation called Germany.

Jamaican soldiers were sent to take part in what became a bloody conflict that lasted for four years, between 1914 and 1918. I was amazed at how many of my black brothers eagerly volunteered to fight for the very colonialists who had suppressed them for so many decades.

I spent many a night sitting in bars, listening for news from over the sea and was saddened to know that many warriors were returning home in wooden boxes.

After the war, in the 1920's and 1930's, harvests began to fail and with pay and conditions worsening a stream of people headed to the cities to find employment. They had little success and the standard of living continued to decline, as ghettos sprang up and began to spore more and more violence.

Then we met a hero who made a great impact on the lot of our black communities throughout the world.

It was on a day of celebration during December 1927.

We were living in Kingston at the time and news had spread that a certain Marcus Garvey was arriving home, having served a prison sentence in the United States. This had been commuted and he had been deported back home to Jamaica, being received by a multitude of his supporters.

We had taken up a vantage point on a large building beside the docks, but when Mister Garvey headed towards his hotel, we followed on behind.

That evening, when all of the excitement had died down, we slipped into his room, to be made welcome by this sturdy built imposing figure of a man.

"Good to see you Mister Anansi. Your reputation precedes you!"

"By the size of the crowd on the dock, you seem to be well known too."

Mister Garvey merely responded with a slow nod of his head, then turned to my wife:

"Hello Missus Anansi. May I call you Crooky?"

"With pleasure Mister Garvey!"

"I gather that you're a freedom fighter, like myself, Anansi."

"Well, I've never thought of myself in exactly that way, but I keep being told that my stories do encourage the use of brain against brawn, so I suppose that does make us comrades."

"Yes! I've followed your adventures since my childhood. How about you telling me a tale."

"I'd love to, provided that you share an adventure or two with Crooky and myself. Have you a favourite story?"

"Well! I remember one my mother told me about Witch Nine and counting yams. I'd love to hear it again."

"So you shall!"

The Nine Yam Hills

You won't believe what happened one day, as I worked in my field.

I was digging around my NINE yam hills, which made me think about a witch who had put a curse on the number nine.

The witch had said that if anyone said nine, they would drop dead.

I don't why I thought about the curse.......... but I did.

Anyway, as I worked, I started to feel hungry and I hadn't brought my dinner with me.

Just at that moment I saw Bredda Goat coming down the lane and I had a vision of curried goat bubbling in a Dutch pot, so I sat down by the yam hills and pretended to cry.

"Why do you cry so, Bredda Anansi?"

Wiping my eyes, I replied:

"I've been trying to count my yam hills all morning, but I can't do it."

"Oh! Silly man! I'll do it for you. One, two, three, four, five, six, seven, eight............ NINE."

Bredda Goat dropped dead.

The curry was delicious.

The next day I was back in the field.

At lunch time I saw Cow coming down the road and had a vision of ox tail soup bubbling in a Dutch pot, so I sat down by the yam hills and pretended to cry.

"Oh dear! What's the problem Bredda Nancy?"

I wiped my eyes and replied:

'...sat down by the yam hills and pretended to cry.'

"I've tried so many times, but I can't count my yam hills."

"Fool! Let me show you how. One, two three, four, five, six, seven, eight........... NINE."

Cow dropped dead.

The oxtail soup was so tasty.

On the third day, who should I see coming down the road at lunch time but Bredda Monkey, and I had a vision of monkey stew bubbling in a Dutch pot.

Monkey stew wasn't my favourite, but it was better than nothing, so I sat down and pretended to cry:

"What on earth are you crying about?"

"I can't count how many yam hills are growing in my field, Bredda Monkey."

"Let me do it for you Anansi. You sit down on yonder yam hill whilst I count. One, two, three, four, five, six, seven, eight....and the one you're sitting on."

I jumped to my feet.

"That's no way to count, Bredda Monkey. Do it again."

So monkey counted again:

"One, two, three, four, five, six, seven, eight..... and the one you were just sitting on."

"NO! NO!" I was vexed now. You don't count like that. You count like this. One, two, three, four, five, six, seven, eight.....NINE."

I dropped dead.

Monkey laughed and pointing his finger said:

"You might fool the others, but you won't fool me."

I'll say no more.

* * * * * * * *

Marcus laughed.

"Wish I could use the 'nine' magic on some of my enemies."

"Enemies?" I questioned. "With the welcome that met you today I can't imagine you having enemies."

"Anansi, I've spent much of my life trying to unite black people around the world and there are those who fear me. Even when I was young, I realised that abolition of slavery was not really the popular agenda for some white folks and improving the lot of black people in Jamaica was considered 'bad' talk.

Crooky and I gave each other a knowing look and we nodded. "Jamaica was still part of the British Empire. English history, language, dress and religion HAD to be our heritage and I remember in school, being taught white man's history and learning that Jamaica was discovered by Columbus .... as though the Arawaks had nothing to do with it. Stories of Captain Morgan and English pirates were more important than Kwaku Ananse or our origins in Africa. Even our economy was geared for the benefit of our white landlords. What Britain decided, was for our own good........ but I can never remember being asked for my opinion. I soon came to realise that this would not change until we had an independent democracy, so I became politically active.

Things became so bad, that unemployment and appalling wages started a wave of departures from our native land, but conditions turned out to be not much better abroad.

I hoped for this trend to be stopped, for skills were in short supply back home. Hope I'm not boring you Anansi?"

"Certainly not Marcus!"

"Well! I've travelled to Africa, Britain and the United States, publishing newspapers to spread the idea of justice for black communities.

I've even stood up for the cause by talking to the crowds who gather at Hyde Park Corner in London. Another time I organised a group of Afro-Americans to resettle, back to their roots in Liberia, but we were turned away. Would you believe it! Turned away by our own ancestors.

We set up and supported black business endeavours, teaching self reliance and to be independent of white monopoly.

We even owned our own shipping line, but this had to wrap up, mainly due to incompetence and corruption amongst our own staff."

I couldn't help but comment:

"Why do we let each other down in that way?"

"I told them.... 'Up you mighty race, you can accomplish what you will,' and they accomplished my being imprisoned for two and a half years."

"Yet you press on?"

"Well, of course. I've survived one assassination attempt, but I can't give up the struggle now, but I tell you this....... I shall never return to America."

"What are your plans for the future then Marcus?"

"I'll be editing a newspaper that I've decided to call 'The Blackman' and with it I hope to help the poor black workers of Jamaica. I might even start a new political party.

"I admire your vision Mister Garvey. I wish you every success in the future, but I think that we've imposed enough on your hospitality. Come now Crooky........time to leave."

Marcus rose hastily from his chair.

"Now Bredda Nancy, I hope you're not thinking of leaving me without telling another story?"

"Very well then. Just one more."

Why Brer Dog Sits and Watches

There was once a time when I was very friendly with Brer Dog.

After a day of hunting, we would often spend the evening under our favourite Cottonwood tree, where I would play my fiddle and Dog accompanied me by raising his head to howl at the moon.

If we didn't catch anything, we would go to Brer Hog's yard looking for scraps of food.

One day we caught nothing and pickings in the yard were very slim, so I suggested to my friend:

"Let's go find a piece of land to rent and grow our own yams. That way we'll never go hungry."

"That sounds very sensible" declared Dog. "The only problem is that I know absolutely nothing about farming."

"Don't fret Brer Dog. I've been growing yam as long as I can remember. I'll teach you how to dig and I'll do the planting."

So we looked around the district until we found a suitable piece of land, agreed a price with the owner, bought two spades and set to work.

I set to with a will and soon I had dug half of the plot, but looking over to Dog, I was amazed to see that he had only turned over three spades full of soil.

"You'll have to do better than that Brer Dog, if you expect to feed off this land."

"Big as my legs Brer Dog."

"Its all right for you Nancy. You're used to this work. I'm finding it very hot and tiring."

"Hard work is the lot of a farmer."

"So you say, but just look at my paws, they're covered in blisters."

"You won't complain Brer Dog, when you're eating your very own roast yam."

"Oh! Very well, but I do hope this hard work will pay off."

"I remember once, when I owned a piece of land just like this one. I grew the most delicious yams that you've ever tasted."

"Were they big Nancy?"

"They were VERY big, Brer Dog."

"How big were they Nancy?"

"Big as my legs Brer Dog."

Well! Everyone knows that my legs are thin and spindly.

"I won't work hard to plant a yam that only grows to the size of one of your legs.   I'd rather sit and watch."

SO! That's why, when you're eating a piece of yam, a dog will be watching you.

That's for sure!

* * * * * * *

Crooky and I talked late into the night.

We both had been deeply impressed by the fervour of this Jamaican man who sought to free the body and spirit of each and every black brother who came under his influence.

We were always glad to hear news of the successes and failures in his fight for black liberation.

He went from strength to strength, some of his followers thinking him to be an invincible prophet, believing that those who opposed him would always come to a bad end.

Alexander Bustamante

Whilst Marcus Garvey was about his international mission of emancipation, two boys had been born and were growing up in the bush, one in the parish of Westmoreland, the other in the parish of Manchester. They were cousins, born nine years apart, and in 1899, they found themselves living together at Belmont in the parish of Clarendon.

The older of these two boys was born and christened Alexander Clarke in 1884.

The younger was born Norman Washington Manley in 1893.

Alexander was later to change his name to Bustamante and between them they were destined to lead Jamaica out of colonial rule.

Later I had the good fortune to meet both of these impressive heroes and discuss their political views.

I met up with the fifty-six year old Alexander Bustamante when the Anansi family were living in the rafters of Up Park Camp in 1940.

He had been arrested for union activities and was to be detained for some time, so I spent many an hour chatting with him and sharing life adventures.

I remember the first time that I slid down from the ceiling, commenting that:

"I seem to spend a lot of time visiting people in prison."

"Oh! Hello Anansi."

"What brings you here then?" I enquired.

"My mouth's been getting me into trouble again."

"Yes, I have the same problem at times. I've been in many a scrape because I can't hold my tongue."

"You too, Anansi? I've always been too outspoken and aggressive for my own good, but I'm not going to stand by whilst my friends have to suffer such bad living conditions."

He smiled a wry smile.

"Since the early 1930's, I've been trying to expose the system by writing to the newspapers and if I say so myself, I've made quite an impact. This has often involved making myself a sacrificial lamb by facing the security forces alone, but being arrested for my beliefs is nothing new.

My cousin Norman is a lawyer of some reputation, so he often helps me to get out of prison, but what does time in prison matter, if one is fighting injustice."

I nodded.

Bustamante continued:

"It was clear that the people needed to be mobilised against our foreign government, so I formed a Labour Union."

"A labour union? What's that?"

"An organisation to allow workers to express their grievances, Anansi."

"About time!"

"I've travelled about a bit in this world and it was so sad to come home and witness the plight of the people."

"Crooky was saying the same thing only the other night."

"Indeed! How is your dear wife?"

"She's very well, thank you sir!"

"Are you both still telling those wonderful stories, Anansi?"

"How could we stop?" I chuckled.

So between our many political exchanges, Alexander insisted that we trade Anansesem, which, of course, I agreed to most willingly.

Here is one that Alexander remembered from his childhood in Clarendon.

When Anansi's House Was In A Tree

'**O**nce, Anansi, Crooky, and their pickney lived high up in a Cotton wood tree, which made them very safe from ma rauders on the ground.

Anansi could roam the countryside, enjoying making mischief and stealing food from here and there, knowing full well that there was a safe refuge up in the branches of his tree.

Tiger had been searching for him.

He often did this, seeking to do Anansi harm.

Well, one particular day, Brer Nancy was foraging around in goat's yard, looking for tasty treats that he could take home to the family, not being aware that Tiger was crouching and watching in the bush close by.

Clutching onto a few morsels for his family, Anansi scampered home and cried up to Crooky':

> "Crooky, dear Crooky! Spin me some line,
> Then pull up some treats for your dinner and mine."

'Unbeknown to Anansi, he had been followed home by Tiger, who now knew where they had their secret tree house.

Off went Tiger, with a big smile on his face, until he arrived at the silversmith's shop.'

"Silversmith, I will pay you well if you can give me a silvery voice."

"Very well," 'said the shopkeeper.' "That will be just one quattie please."

"Crooky, dear Crooky! Spin me some line..."

'So off went Tiger to the Cotton tree and standing below he began to sing in his new silvery voice':

"Crooky, dear Crooky! Spin me some line,
Then pull up some treats for your dinner and mine."

'Now Crooky was not deceived by this, crying down':

"That's not the smooth voice of my husband. Go away!"

'So off went Tiger, but without a smile on his face, until he arrived at the goldsmith's shop.'

"Goldsmith, I will pay you well, if you can give me a golden voice."

"Very well." 'said the shopkeeper' "That will be just two quatties please."

'So off went Tiger again and standing below the cotton tree, he began to sing with a lisp in his new golden voice':

"Crooky, dear Crooky! Spin me some line,
Then pull up some treats for your dinner and mine."

'So good was the imitation, that Crooky believed that her husband was standing below, so spinning some line she lowered it down to the ground.

Tiger, with a smile back on his face, began to climb up.

He heaved his heavy body, hand over hand, up the sticky line.

Closer and closer he came to the Anansi residence.

Suddenly, Anansi came running from the bush, having just returned from Brer Dog's yard and cried in a loud voice':

"Crooky! It's a trick! Cut the line! Cut the line!"

'So Missus Anansi cut the line.

Tiger fell.

Tiger broke his neck.

Anansi, Crooky and the pickney had tiger meat for dinner.

Don't you think that Anansi is the smartest of them all?'

I couldn't help but to agree with him.

* * * * * * *

My family and I kept Mister Bustamante company during his imprisonment.

He had talked about his cousin Norman Manley and painted such a picture of a man with great convictions, that we decided to visit him as soon as our friend Alexander was released from prison.

A new war had been raging between Great Britain and Germany since 1939. It seemed that these two nations didn't get on very well and eventually most major powers found themselves drawn into these terrible hostilities, Jamaica once again providing soldiers to aid the commonwealth volunteers.

During these desperate years, we received sad news that our acquaintance Marcus Garvey had died in London.

In 1943 we went looking for Norman Manley and found him in his office at the Headquarters of the Peoples National Party.

"Hope you don't mind us dropping down on you like this, Mister Manley?"

"Never too busy to meet you and your wife, Anansi. Take a seat. What can I do for you?"

"We were talking to your cousin at the Up Park Camp recently and when we mentioned that your work interested us, he suggested that we look you up."

Mister Manley laughed and replied:

"What you could possibly find interesting about my exertions, I can't imagine, but fire away with whatever you'd like to know."

"Crooky and I have always been concerned about the welfare of the people and things haven't been going too well lately. Alexander says that you, like him, wish things would change."

"You're right on the mark there, Anansi! Although I've been successful in my own life, did well at school, became a teacher, went to Oxford University, survived the First Word War, have been awarded the Military Medal and have since been successful as a lawyer, I've always empathised with the working men and women of my homeland, so in 1938 I founded the P.N.P to fight for a fairer system. Cousin Alexander has been busy building his union, the Bustamante Industrial

Norman Manley

Trade Union and seems to enjoy being placed in detention for his beliefs. I help him as best I can. My politics are more to the 'left' than his, but we do see eye to eye that things can't really improve until we stand as an independent nation, in control of our own destiny.

Busta tells me that he intends to form his own party, the Jamaica Labour Party. That'll liven things up!"

I became quite excited at the idea.

Mister Manley shrugged and continued:

"I'm aware that our farmers are travelling to America, to work in the fruit fields over there. What a poor state of affairs, when they can't find useful, well paid employment back home"

"True!"

"Alex told me of your visits and your exchanges of the old tales whilst he was in Up Park. I hope that you will do me the same honour."

"I don't see why not, Mister Manley."

"Norman will do."

"Thank you. Anyway, you sit comfortably and I'll tell you of the time I had a problem with Fire."

Norman sat back, placed his hands behind his head, closed his eyes and leaned back on his desk chair.

The Problem I Had with Fire

here was a time when Fire and I were very good friends.

I would often take my Dutch pot and a nice piece of beef or some chicken legs around to his yard, and Fire would burn under the Dutch pot to cook up supper. When my belly was full, we would sit up all hours, chatting about this and that.

On each occasion when I left to make my way home, I would say to Fire:

"You really must come round to my yard some time. Crooky would be most pleased to see you!"

He always replied:

"I'd love to, but I can't walk."

Each enjoyable night in Fire's company, I threw out the same invitation for him to pay us a visit, but he always replied with the same:

"I'd love to, but I can't walk."

When I arrived home I said to Crooky:

"I feel bad that Fire can't come to visit."

Crooky was quick to reply:

"Don't invite him, husband! He will only bring us mischief."

"Don't talk nonsense, woman. Fire is my best friend."

The following week I suggested an idea that would allow Fire to visit our yard:

'Fire continued to burn up the porch...'

"You say that you can't walk, but if I lay a trail of dry plantain trash to my front door, you should be able to burn your way along it and pay us a visit."

So the next evening, I did just that, carefully laying a trail of dry trash all the way to my door.

"Come along friend! Just burn along this trail and we'll have supper with Crooky tonight."

So he did, burning across his front garden, out into the lane, following the trash all the way to my yard. He burned through the gate, across my garden and up the steps onto my porch.

Crooky saw trouble coming, so she ran out of the back door.

Fire continued to burn up the porch, then carried right on into the house.

He burnt up my lovely home.

He made me jump, but I couldn't escape, so I was burned up too.

Fire burned up every thing except my wife.

Fire certainly fooled me.

Would you believe that I could get into so much trouble?

* * * * * * *

Alexander Bustamante did indeed form his Jamaica Labour Party, which he presented to the nation at the first General Election in 1944. Standing face to face against his cousin Norman Manley and the People's National Party he won with a large majority, becoming the Premier of Jamaica for the next ten years.

The Great War ended in 1945.

Yet again, our service men and women came home to find a depressed economy, with little on offer as reward for their fight for king and country.

I was later to discover, that on the 6th of February in that same year, a significant new star had arrived in Jamaica.

A certain Cedella Booker had given birth to a boy child, who she named Robert Nesta Marley.

I'm sad to say that our paths were never to cross.

In the meantime our family wandered around Kingston, taking up residence wherever the pickings looked most attractive.

It was the evening of the 23rd of May 1948 and we were all living in an old warehouse close by the docks. I was outside, on the third storey of this currently empty building, spinning a web under a window sill. As I scurried from thread to thread, I had an excellent view of the street below and couldn't help but notice scores of people, all heading in the same direction, each one carrying a suitcase or a large brown paper parcel under an arm.

"What happens?"

My curiosity drew me down to the ground and I followed them to a ship that was berthed in the shelter of the warehouse wall.

Making my way to the hawser that tied the vessel to the quay side, I started to climb up to the bows, where I was intending to board. As I ascended, I noticed that the name of the steamship was the Empire Windrush and my later eavesdropping informed me that she was a re-tired troopship, due to sail to England the following day.

Wandering around the sleeping quarters, I listened for information that would tell me why nearly five hundred of my fellow Jamaicans were travelling to a land far from home. I settled on a bunk near to a group of domino playing men and spied on their conversation.

"What brings you here, friend?" said a double-six holder.

"I read a press article that said that England was a land of opportunity for ex-service men and women, so I'm off to see for myself." He smiled and responded with a six-five.

"Me too! Things haven't been too good since I came back from the war, so I've decided to find that gold that paves the streets of 'Old Blighty.' Double five."

"Yep." laughed another, slamming down a five-two."

The fourth player paused to contemplate his 'hand', then the five-blank domino hit the table with such force, that the ship seemed to rock on its moorings.

"My family are staying behind. Hope they're going to be all right!"

"Well, they can't be any worse off than mine have been these last three years."

This last remark brought the game to a temporary standstill and the group sat motionlessly contemplating the lot of their loved ones. An air of gloom was settling around the cabin, until someone spoke out:

"Now then lads, let's not get depressed about leaving family. They can always follow on later."

"Sure! I know. Lets tell a few tales to cheer us up? Anyone know any stories about Anansi, the Spiderman?"

One of the older men volunteered and soon laughter replaced the unease that was evident amongst the Windrush pioneers.

Amazingly the game was put to one side, and if you know Jamaican men and their love for dominoes, one would likely say that I had just witnessed a miracle.

A voice rang down the cabin:

"Gather round boys and I'll weave you a yarn about Brer Nancy."

Brer Anansi, Tiger and Rat

Jackanory, I'll tell you a story.

One day Brer Nancy and Brer Rat went for a pleasant stroll in the bush, each of them carrying a basket to collect fruits that had fallen from the trees.

They weren't having much luck and decided to head for home, when they saw four tiger cubs playing amongst the roots of a Cotton-wood tree.

Anansi said to Rat':

"Good! We won't go home empty handed. Crooky will cook tiger cub pie for supper tonight" 'and picking up a pup, he PRETENDED to kill it, then put it in his basket.'

"What a good idea Nancy" 'said Rat, picking up a pup, KILLING it and putting it in his basket.

Looking in his basket Anansi commented':

"There's not much meat on this little pup, so I think I'll take another one for my pickney."

'He took up another pup, PRETENDED to kill it and placed it alongside its brother.'

"I've got a large family to feed." 'agreed Rat' "I'll take another one as well." 'and collecting up another pup, he KILLED it and put it in his basket.

95

'...roaring at rat to come out...'

Just then Tiger came running towards the tree.

Looking in Anansi's basket, Tiger roared':

"Where do you think you're going with my puppies?"

"Your pickneys were lost and hungry, so we collected them up and we were on our way to find you, Bredda Tiger."

Tiger stopped roaring and swishing his tail and purred:'

"That's so kind Nancy. Give them to me and I'll take them home for some supper."

'Tiger collected up his two children and hugged them close.'

"I left four of them playing together. Have you seen the other two."

'By this time, Brer Rat was shaking and trying to slip away to hide.'

"Indeed! Bredda Tiger. You'll find them in Rat's basket."

Tiger lifted the two pups from Rat's basket and hugged them up.

"Why are my children so cold?" 'said Tiger anxiously, then sniffing at them he realised that they were dead.

All of the animals for miles around shook as they heard Tiger's roar of anguish.

He turned on Rat to kill him, but Brer Rat made a hasty getaway, dodging back and forwards to avoid the grasping claws of a now furious beast. Rat headed for a derelict old house, running close to the wall and squealing to Anansi:'

"Save me Nancy, save me!"

"Rat, look for a stone hole." 'Anansi shouted.'

"Why do I need a stone hole, Nancy?"

"To escape into, you silly rat."

'Rat understood and seeing a hole in the stone wall, he raced towards it, with Tiger rushing close behind. As Tiger's claws were about to sink into his flank, rat scuttled into the safety of the cavity. Tiger prowled backwards and forwards, clawing at the hole and roaring for Rat to come out to be punished.

But Rat never came out.

That's why Rat is fond of stone holes and that's where you'll find him to this very day.

Jack Mandora. I'll say no more.'

* * * * * * *

We stood on the dock the following day, waving the Empire Windrush good bye and praying that my Lord Nyame would look over these intrepid souls.

I was to learn later that many did well for themselves, even though there wasn't the welcome they expected. In spite of having fought for King and Commonwealth, the British government were keen to send them back home and they had to suffer the indignity of signs in the windows of places to rent that blatantly declared "NO COLOUREDS, NO DOGS."

My own disappointment, however, was to know that Jamaica was losing its valuable craftsmen and experienced workers, who were sorely needed back home to build up the sagging economy.

This trend was to increase, as more of our most valuable assets decided that emigrating was their only solution to poverty.

Alexander Bustamante received a Knighthood from the Queen, but the following year his party had to step down to the Peoples Nationalist Party and his cousin Norman Manley.

By now Norman was beginning to advocate a Federation of West Indian Islands, to form a 'Common Market', that hoped to allow the Caribbean Islands to be economically more independent, and less under the control of major capitalist nations, but this was opposed by Bustamante and the idea was eventually thrown out by a National Referendum.

By the time we had asked Great Britain for Independence in 1961, we had lost some 113.000 people, all seeking better conditions abroad.

The rot was well under way.

During this period the P.N.P. was returned to power and Robert Nesta Marley began his professional singing career with his band, the Rudeboys, but not meeting with much success he returned to Trench Town.

Then the year 1962 arrived and what an eventful year it turned out to be.

At midnight on the 5th August, Jamaica was granted its Independence and Bustamante became the first Prime Minister of the island, having regained power at the General Election.

I remember being in the new National Stadium with Crooky and the boys, to witness the ceremonies.

We sat underneath the seat of Her Royal Highness Princess Margaret, who was with her husband, the Earl of Snowden and our first Governor General Sir Kenneth Blackburne.

Guests from all over the world witnessed the raising of the Jamaican flag.

Then we had the fright of our lives.

The Stadium exploded with a violent sound, greater than that made by the God of Thunder. Streaks of fire rose high into the night sky, bursting in great cloud shaking eruptions, that sent cascades of crackling multicoloured fire showering from the heavens.

My family trembled in terror.

We had never seen a fireworks display before and it was a while before we realised that the people were making this commotion just for fun.

It was long into the morning before the street partying began to tire and the following night saw us sitting in the yard of a weary family, who were sharing with us their feelings and apprehensions about the newly gained independence.

Grandfather had bitter memories of the struggles that had led to this freedom and he said to me:

"Surely you'll be glad to see true freedom at last, Anansi."

"Indeed I will Grandpa. It's been a long time coming and I'm still concerned for my people. There's still too much poverty."

"Indeed Anansi, but let us not dwell on that tonight. Its time to celebrate..........

.... who's going to tell us a story?"

Brer Rooster Tricks Anansi

This is how it began.

A man had a daughter, who was renowned throughout the land for her beauty.

Bredda Rooster and Brer Anansi both fell in love with her and began to compete for her affections.

One day Anansi called on Rooster and suggested that':

"We are both taken with the same man's daughter, so let's both go to see the father to ask for her hand and let the best man win."

"Very well." 'Rooster responded.

Bredda Rooster was most happy to take up this challenge, because he knew that with his coloured feathers and bright red cockscomb, he was by far the most handsome of all the creatures around.

Anansi would have no chance at all.

So the following day, Anansi told Bredda Rooster to meet him on the lane, so that they could walk together to the man's yard.'

"Please give me an early call, Bredda Rooster, then we can meet straight after breakfast."

"Very well, Anansi."

'True to his word, Rooster crowed loudly the following morning.

Anansi woke up, dressed quickly and set off to the man's yard, not bothering to have breakfast or wait for Rooster.

'...Rooster crowded loudly...'

When he arrived, he started to make his case as a suitor, but the man said':

"Fine Brer Anansi, I've heard your case, but we must wait for Bredda Rooster, who is also interested in my daughter."

"Oh, Brother Rooster is of no-account. He's a lazy fellow, who couldn't even get here on time."

'At that moment, Bredda Rooster came in the gate, apologised to the man, explaining how he had been tricked into being so late. The man was sympathetic and listened to him make his case.'

"Right!" pronounced the man. "I've listened to your speeches and I find it difficult to decide, so I tell you what! The first of you to arrive in my yard after sunrise tomorrow can have my daughter's hand in marriage."

'As he walked home, Brer Anansi decided to be up at the first crow of Bredda Rooster and race to be first, but his rival had already made a plan of his own.

Bredda Rooster didn't sleep that night, NOR did he CROW at sunrise. In fact, as the sun peeped over the horizon, he was already waiting outside the man's gate.

Poor Anansi didn't wake up at cockcrow, because the cock didn't crow, did it?

Anansi overslept.

When he finally got out of bed, he rushed to claim his bride, but he only arrived at the man's yard in time for Rooster's wedding.

So the early Rooster caught the......... lady.

Rooster did it!'

* * * * * * *

Bob Marley, who was living not far from where we were listening to this story of trickery was getting ready to enter the music business again and soon was releasing hit after hit record. He was to give his band the new name of 'The Wailers' and make reggae music popular, singing songs about things he knew so well...... poverty, peace, love and liberty.

In the year of the anniversary of Morant Bay, a certain Martin Luther King received the Keys of the City of Kingston.

Yes! Martin Luther King, that famed freedom fighter from America, who preached passive resistance against racism.

He believed in political action without violence, using the same methods adopted by a certain Mahatma Gandhi in India, another country that suffered under colonial rule.

As I thought about the speech that he made at our University, my mind was drawn back to my good friend Sam Sharpe and the lessons he tried so hard to teach about non-violence. Ghandi and King were merely continuing a concept that had been laid down by one of our own heroes all those years ago.

Interesting how all of these gallant men were ultimately killed by men of violence.

Even Bob, in spite of his peaceful Rastafarian views about oppression and inequality nearly fell victim to gunmen.

Early in 1966 I was witness to a state visit by His Imperial Majesty Emperor Haile Selassie I of Ethiopia, King of Kings, Lord of Lords, Conquering Lion of the Tribe of Judah, Elect of God, Light of the World, King of Zion, Restorer of the Dynasty of Solomon.

I wondered what his friends called him?

Waiting high in a coconut tree beside the road as his cavalcade passed close by, it gave me an excellent view of his Majesty. Sitting in an open topped motor vehicle, this black bearded, weather worn dignitary was immaculate in a grey uniform, festooned with medals. A black military belt circled his waist and a pith helmet protected his royal head from the glaring sun.

Before his Coronation, he was known as Ras Tafari, and as many Jamaicans believed him to be their long awaited Messiah, they had taken upon themselves the name Rastafarians.

I came to understand the link between the prophetic thoughts of Marcus Garvey, the cry of the people to reunite with their roots in Africa and Sellassie's belief that many 'Jamaicans and Ethiopians were brothers by blood'.

It was this visit that prompted me to spend time mixing with these people of the 'dreadlocks', finding them to be without anger, full of love, needing little in the way of material possessions and carrying a spirit for freedom that reminded me of my good friend Nanny.

It was during the year of this state visit that Bob Marley became a Rastafarian.

Anyway the visit went rather well.

Marley married Rita Anderson and left for America.

This also went well.

The body of Marcus Garvey was brought from England and enshrined back home.

This went very well.

During the four weeks of October, a State of Emergency was declared in Kingston, due to escalating violence by political gangs. People were being shot and stabbed and my friends killed each other in the street for no good reason.

This was not well at all.

Surely this was not the intended fruits sown by our Jamaican heroes.

It was with sadness that my friend Bustamante retired the following year and he said to me one evening as we talked over old times:

"I needed to be a militant man to battle against Colonial rule, but I'm sorry that emancipation and political freedom has led to violence on the streets of Kingston.

"Yes Alex.! My sentiment."

"Well, I've done all that I can for the nation. I can do no more!"

"All I can say Alex, is that I hope your pioneering work won't be forgotten!" I comforted.

Bustamante laughed.

"I shall never attain the fame of your good self, Anansi."

"I wouldn't be too sure about that. People don't tell my stories like they used to do."

"Come now Anansi, that's a depressing thing to say."

"Not really Alex, the old ways are soon forgotten."

"Come now, such sadness will never do. You need some cheering up. How about swapping a few tales."

"O.K."

How Green Lizard Earned His Stripes

O nce upon a time I was strolling home from the village and was near a house that I passed most days.

On this particular occasion, I was attracted to the sound of singing...... the most beautiful singing that I'd ever heard.

Stopping beside the yard wall, I climbed up and peeped over and there, in the garden, a beautiful girl was crouching over a bowl of sudsy water, singing and washing clothes.

My heart went out to her and I knew that I was in love.

"Beautiful maiden." I called "I wish to court and marry you."

"Kind sir. You will need to ask my mother."

"Come out mother. I wish to marry your daughter!"

A large woman strode out onto the verandah and with legs apart and folded arms, she raised her head and laughed.":

"NO WAY! No man will marry my daughter unless he can discover her name."

So I started to guess.

"Patrice, Patience, Ebony, Louise, Mary, Catherine or might it be Felicity?"

Her mother laughed until her hips shook.

"Shantelle, Betty, Maureen, Charity, Bernice, Monique or could it be Joy?"

Mother had to sit down from laughing.

"Who's messed up the clothes again?"

I guessed all afternoon, but with no success, so had to admit defeat and leave the maiden's yard.

"What's the matter, Brer Anansi? You look so sad!"

Turning towards the voice, I saw Green Lizard, lying still on the branch of a tree.

"My very good friend Green Lizard. I can use your help."

"Certainly not Anansi. You'll probably trick me."

"I promise not to trick you and if you help me I'll give you a present."

"Very well then." agreed Lizard and walking into the mother's yard, he muddied himself up, then walked all over the newly washed clothes that had been laid out to dry.

"Oh! my goodness! Who's messed up the clothes?"

Mother set to, to wash them over again.

She laid them out to dry, but as soon as she went in the house, Lizard walked all over them again.

"Oh! my goodness! Who's messed up the clothes again?" and she set to, to wash them yet again.

As she went into the house, Green Lizard made muddy footprints all over the third wash.

This time mother came out and seeing the clothes dirtied up, she angrily cried out:

"ROSALIA! ROSALIA! Someone keeps messing up your washing!"

Green Lizard scampered off to bring me the name of the beautiful young maiden.

So I went back to the house singing:

"Rosalia! Rosalia! I'm coming to marry you."

Rosalia ran in to her mother calling:

"Mamma! Mamma! My lover is coming to marry me."

"He cannot." said mother angrily. "He doesn't know your name."

I swaggered in the gate, singing;

"Your daughter's name is ROSALIA."

Mother was thunderstruck, but she had to give me the hand of her daughter.

I asked my Father Nyame to give Lizard a present.

Lizard was given dark green stripes on his back.

He was well pleased.

* * * * * *

To confirm my anxieties about the state of the democracy there was major civil disorder during August of 1968, when one person was killed and millions of Jamaican dollars of damage was caused.

Soon after Norman Manley resigned as Leader of the Opposition. When I asked him if the growing unrest was behind his withdrawal, he evaded my question. Eight months later my good friend was dead.

Maybe he knew?

Things were not all sorrow, however, for October 20th was established as National Heroes Day and during that month their were Military parades and celebrations.

Granny Nanny was not yet officially recognised as a heroine, but this was to happen in 1975.

In 1970, statues of Bustamante and Manley were unveiled

Bob Marley was writing songs for Johnny Nash.

At the next General Election the P.N.P was led to a landslide victory by Norman's son Michael and then began a battle of ideologies, that seethed for ten years.

I had met Michael at one of the story telling sessions that I'd had from time to time with his father, so I paid him a visit.

During one of my friendly meetings with Michael, he expressed concern for his beloved Jamaica.

"Anansi! I have a dilemma in resolving the bad state of financial affairs in the country. We don't seem to be getting a fair deal by remaining in the Commonwealth. The people have already stated that they don't want to have economic connections with other West Indians and America is not a safe bet. Our only friend seems to be Castro in Cuba.

"Isn't he what they call a Communist?"

"So they say Anansi, but I'm not holding that against him. I don't want to embrace his dogma, but Castro is the only world leader, so far, who is offering our country practical help without strings attached."

"In what way?"

"Well, he says that he is prepared to send doctors to help in our hospitals and engineers to improve the roads. He will build new schools and educate our higglers to be more successful in the markets."

"Well, that seems better than getting into debt."

"Right, Anansi. I want the people to WORK towards a more Socialist prosperity and if we're ever to rise out of the current economic doldrums that we're in at present, it will require a great deal of hard effort."

"Do you think that the people will respond? They never responded to Marcus."

"They might, if I can stop our assets being creamed off by imperialists from abroad, who still act like our white slave masters of old, controlling our nation with their money, skimming off our wealth and taking all of our best resources.

"The Rastas call them Babylon" said I.

"I may have to nationalise our industries and place them in the hands of the nation." continued Michael.

"Look what happened when Marcus bought the shipping line!"

"I know its risky Anansi, but we must try a new approach to redirect our energy from civil disorder into a 'self help' policy that may build up a proud nation."

"I wish you every success Michael. Must go! Be seeing you!"

"Hold on Anansi! You can't leave without a story. Father told me of the wonderful stories that you collect and it's a long time since I heard one. Do me the honour before you leave.!

"Very well!"

Michael sat back, placed his hands behind his head, closed his eyes and leaned back on the desk chair.

He did remind me of his father.

Tiger's Bone Hole

One day I was walking close by Tiger's house.

Tiger had been hunting and was returning with a large cow, that he had probably killed and stolen from a farmer.

Hiding in a tree I watched as he dragged it into his yard, skinned it, put it up on a spit, lit a fire and slowly turned it until the fat dripped and sizzled in the flames.

When it was cooked to perfection, Tiger cut it up, put it in a large bowl, which he placed on the verandah.

Then he set off to work in his field, intending to eat the cow meat for his supper.

As soon as I saw him busy at work, I rushed home to find Crooky and the boys:

"Come Crooky! I've found us a free dinner."

Off we went, found the beef, set to to enjoy a feast, but it wasn't long before Tiger came home from his field.

"Hide! Hide!"

"Where shall we hide?"

Well, Tiger had dug a big hole in the garden, where he threw the bones after he had eaten all of the meat from them.

"Quick!" I cried. "Hide in the bone hole!"

So dashing across the yard, we dived helter-skelter into the deep hole and hid amongst the old bones.

'*...the missile struck Doshey on the head.*'

We heard Tiger open the gate, stroll to the verandah and settle down for his feast.

"Somebody's been at my beef," grumbled Tiger.

We peeped over the edge, to watch him tearing at the juicy meat with his knifelike teeth, when suddenly, he threw a stripped bone towards the hole, causing us to duck, but the missile struck Doshey on the head.

He was just about to holler, but I leapt on him and stifled his yell.

"Shush!" I whispered. "If Tiger discovers us, he'll eat us all for sure."

Tiger finished off another piece and threw the bone down the hole, hitting Takuma on the elbow.

"Shut your mouth, Takuma! Don't cry!"

Another bone came flying through the air and cracked Crooky right on the knee.

She nearly called out in pain.

The last bone caught me right in the middle of my back, knocking me down, so I muttered:

"Right! Enough is enough!" and turning to the family I asked:

"When I give the signal, I want everyone to scream out.

So we all shrieked together at the top of our voices:

"Yee! Yee... e.e.e.e.e.e.e!"

Tiger was nearly frightened to death.

He ran away crying:

"The duppies have come to get me!"

My family came out of the bone hole and we took all of the meat home.

We ate cow meat for days and days.

What do you think of that?"

* * * * * * *

The policies of the P.N.P and the Labour Party began to polarize, their doctrinal differences festering, so that it became difficult to travel about safely in the Kingston ghettos, as rival political gangs took to gun fighting in the streets.

To declare your political beliefs in the wrong place, at the wrong time, to the wrong person could have you beaten, stabbed or even shot, so I decided to take my family back into the bush, where I thought we would be safe from the 'Rude Boys' and the street disputes.

We took up residence in the rafters of a bar and would often listen in to the many 'debates' that the punters had most nights, as they consumed a few cans of Red Stripe beer.

One particular night, I was particularly intrigued by an animated conversation, between three local farmers.

"I tell you man, we're being poisoned."

"Poisoned, how do you mean poisoned?"

"It's true man. All of my coconut and banana trees are dying and I can't account for it!"

"Well now!" interjected the third man. "Now that you mention it, I'm having problems as well and Robert was saying only the other day that Ferguson's plantation was looking sick."

"Someone's trying to sabotage our agriculture."

"It's those damn Yankies, you know! Since Manley has been shaking hands with Castro, they've really been trying to sabotage our economy."

"Yes! I wouldn't be at all surprised if their secret service hasn't been spraying our crops with something."

"Rubbish man. They wouldn't dare!"

"Well something strange is 'appening, that's for sure!"

"Isn't that funny! I was chatting with the community nurse yesterday and she said the same thing. She's concerned at the number of cases she's seeing with a condition that she calls 'pink eye,' that she can't account for. She says that the whole community seems lethargic, as though they've been poisoned." "You see, that's no coincidence I tell you. Those Americans want us to fail."

"Difficult to prove."

"Indeed, but I wouldn't be surprised."

Whether there was any substance to this rural myth, would indeed be difficult to prove, but it was true that the United States bullied and squeezed our economy during these radical years.

The P.N.P. declared, around this time, that its philosophy was 'Democratic Socialist,' to stave off the rumours that it was going Communist.

Following a military coup during August, 1975, Haile Sellassie died. It was rumoured that he had been assassinated.

In 1976, Bob Marley planned to hold a free Peace Concert at Kingston's National Heroes Park on the 5th December.

This was his effort to pour oil on the troubled waters of the democratic process, that had deteriorated into further bloody gun battles in the slum areas of the city.

At the same time it was announced that the government intended to hold a General Election just fifteen days later.

All hell broke loose.

Just before the concert, gunmen attempted to assassinate Bob, but he was only wounded and was rushed into the Blue Mountain area for safety.

So much for his call for peace.

There were those who clearly had no intention of being like their god Jesus.

Things were so bad, that a state of national emergency was called and hundreds of people were detained.

My decision to take the family out of the city for safety was well founded.

Bob showed his courage in the face of this danger, by still holding the concert, but what a shame that his plea for brotherhood and unity had failed.

Afterwards he didn't perform in his bleeding homeland for a long time, seeking safety in London, England.

The election returned Michael to power.

The following year, my dear 93 year old friend Alexander joined his cousin in their heaven.

He tried so hard, but now his place was taken by a certain Edward Seaga.

I sorely missed our occasional exchanges of Anansesem.

Bob came home in 1978, to deliver a One Love Peace Concert before Michael and Edward, as a final effort to put balm on the festering wounds of political rivalry and he persuaded Seaga and Manley to shake hands on stage, as a symbolic gesture of unity.

When I heard the news of this monumental step to reunite my people, I brought the family back, into what I thought was a newly safe Kingston.

Mistake! Mistake!

By the middle of 1980, some three hundred deaths had resulted from street violence, amongst whom nearly a dozen policemen were killed.

When would it cease?

My people had abandoned the old religion long ago, to adopt the god of their oppressors.

They welcomed this Jesus and took him to their hearts.

On many occasions, I sat in a web, high up in the beams of a chapel, listening to the teaching of this man from Galilee.

He had become dear to me, because he also taught about freedom, a very profound freedom, that could release his followers from sin and even death.

Like Sam Sharpe, Martin Luther King and Muhatma Ghandi, this Jesus taught the idea of passive resistance and non-violence and even allowed himself to be crucified rather than call his hosts from heaven to intervene on his behalf.

I had some difficulty understanding how my people could nod their heads when the preacher talked about 'offering the other cheek,' then walk from the church to be intolerant, bigoted and violent towards their 'brothers and sisters'.

Why do my people take their politics so seriously, that it must lead to bloodshed?

Where's that brotherly love that they talk about?

One night at home, I felt so low , as I brooded on the hypocrisy of it all.

"My dear husband." soothed Crooky. "What ails thee? You seem so sad."

I sat with her and she held my hands as I shared my unhappiness caused by the failure of my hopes, desires and expectations for my Jamaican friends.

I had also begun to wonder about my own identity and the things I believed.

I appealed to Crooky.

"Am I a hypocrite as well?"

"What on earth do you mean, my love?"

"Well, I've been scolding my people for being violent, yet some of the tricks that I have played on my friends and enemies, were often very naughty."

"I understand your feelings Anansi, but remember that it was your Father Nyame who sent you to earth with a mission."

"A mission Crooky! What do you mean?"

"You've said so yourself, that your stories are to teach mankind not to submit to tyranny."

"Well! I suppose you're right, but some of the tricks that I have pulled have been uncaring, to say the least. I've killed and eaten Brer Tiger, Brer Monkey, Brer Goat and Brer Cow." Crooky laughed.

"Well! Of course. The stories required that you do so, but they ALWAYS come back to life, ready for the next tale."

"Maybe so, but I've also betrayed and stolen from my friends, and I've even tricked my own son Takuma."

"Do they not still love you and boast of your cunning? Remember that they're only STORIES Anansi and in folk tales nobody comes to any REAL harm."

"You're a great comfort, my dear Crooky, but I wonder whether my people do indeed still love me? They don't tell Anansesem as they once did."

"Well! Your wife and pickney love you for sure."

"Bless you, Aso!" It was nice to use her name of endearment.

"Now, my husband, you're being a right grumble belly tonight, so I think we'll have to cheer you up. What if I tell one of your naughty adventures?"

Starting to feel more cheerful, I settled back in the web to enjoy the narrative that followed:

The Sheepskin Suit

'I wonder if you remember the time, my husband, when you went to work for Mr Grandman?

He had hundreds and hundreds of sheep and he was looking for some hardworking person to mind them.

I remember well that nobody applied for the job and when you went along Mr Grandman said':

"Well! I suppose you'll have to do."

She gave me a cheeky wink, for she knew (so did Mr Grandman) that I always preferred to be swinging on my hammock in the shade, than working under the hot sun.

'You hadn't been working for him for more than a week, when sheep began to go missing, one at a time and I noticed that we were eating mutton more often than usual.'

"Where are my sheep going, Anansi? You're supposed to be looking after them."

"I really don't know," you said to Mr Grandman. "I suspect that someone is stealing them in the night."

"Well, we must put a stop to it, so I'll give you one hundred guineas if you catch the thief."

'Well, about that time, Mr Goodman was planning to hold his Annual Ball, so you suggested that you could provide the dance music and set a trap for the thief.

You went to see Bredda Tiger, to ask if he would play the drums in your band. He agreed, so you also asked him to help you to catch the sheep thief.

"It's true, friends, it's true..."

I remember that you said to Tiger:'

"Friend Tiger. If you come to the Ball as yourself, you're sure to frighten the guests, so kindly wear these sheepskin clothes and you gave him a coat, trousers, hat and shoes."

'You spent all week practising a new dance tune and song that went as follows:'

"Mr Grandman has lost all of his flock.

I wonder if Tiger has taken the lot?"

'Then you went to Tiger and flattered':

"Brer Tiger, you have such a wonderful singing voice, I wonder if you would honour me, by helping me to sing a new song, that I have written specially for the Ball?"

'Tiger puffed up with the flattery, agreed at once, so you taught him to sing':

"It's true, friends, it's true.

Where else would I get these clothes, so new!"

'Mr Grandman had sent out invitations to all of his rich friends and on the night of the Grand Ball, they all came in fine carriages, wearing their finest clothes.

You tuned up your fiddle:

Ge-ang, De-ang, Ae-ang, Ee-ang.

Tiger tuned up his drums:

Bum-dum, Dum-dum, Rum-dum, Pum-dum.

Then you stood up and called to one and all':

"Take your partners and I'll sing you a song

Then you can promenade all night long."

'You played the fiddle, Brer Goat strummed the guitar, Brer Monkey picked the banjo, Brer Tortoise twanged the jew's harp and Tiger beat the drums and you began to sing':

"Mr Grandman has lost all of his flock.

I wonder if Tiger has taken the lot?"

'Then Tiger, without thinking, joined in with':

"It's true, friends, it's true.

Where else would I get these clothes, so new?"

'Mr Grandman stopped the dance and with a shout of triumph, pointed at Tiger:'

"There's the thief that stole my sheep!"

"No! Not me." 'roared Tiger.

You jumped off the bandstand, pointing at Tiger:'

"Yes! He's the thief who ate all the sheep. Breeda Tiger, how could you do such a terrible thing?"

'Tiger was put in chains and dragged away and you were given the one hundred guineas reward.

You are a wicked fellow, but I can't help but like you!'

* * * * * * *

A few years before, unbeknown to many, Bob Marley had hurt his foot, whilst playing football.

Like the ghetto violence, the injury had festered and belated treatment discovered it to be cancerous and treatment in the U.S.A was without success. By the time that Bob was giving his last tour in Zimbabwe, at an Independence Celebration, the canker had spread throughout his body.

During this premature twilight phase of his life, he was presented with the Medal of Peace by the United States and Jamaica's Order of Merit.

He battled hard to overcome, but finally succumbed and died in Miami on Monday the 11th of May, 1981.

Crooky and I were filled with great sorrow.

My ambition to meet this remarkable emissary for peace was not to be.

All that my family and I could do to show respect, was to follow the cortege to his burial at Nine Mile.

Bob was only 36 years old when he died, but he achieved more in the cause for peace, than many men accomplish in a life time twice as long.

Half of the population of our island flocked to his funeral, but he has still not yet been added to the names of our Jamaican Heroes.

Like Nanny, he may have to wait another century and a half to be so honoured.

His memory lingered on, but his message for peace and unity, was by and large ignored, for the poison of violence still bubbled up in the slums of Kingston.

The message of Robert and your god Jesus still fell on stony ground.

The British Queen Elizabeth and her husband, the Duke of Edinburgh visited the island in 1983.

During that year Michael did NOT contest at the General Election, to allow Edward and the J.L.P. to have all of the seats in the house of government.

The economy continued to slide down a bumpy road of recession.

In 1989, Michael regained power, but in spite of more moderate policies, things did not greatly improve.

Many of our precious resources were still migrating abroad.

It is as though the nation had a death wish.

My energy began to fail and I felt that I soon must die, but when I return to my father Nyame, I shall take with me the memory and privilege of having met yet another great fighter for peace and unity, for in the month of July in the year of 1991, a certain South African, Nelson Rolihlahla Mandela visited the island, to tumultuous applause and was given an Honorary Degree.

My waning curiosity was revived when I was in a local bar, hearing him being referred to as a fighter for racial equality. Seeking him out at his hotel, I used my guile to sneak into his room to introduce myself.

I thought that my cup was overflowing when he told me his life story.

With the passing of Bob, I had assumed that the vision for freedom would die, but I was forgetting that all over the world many nations and peoples were seeking their just share of liberty.

"Nice to meet you, Mister Anansi. I believe that we're both African."

"I come from further north than yourself, Mister Mandela."

"Yes! I'm familiar with the Ashanti nation and their folk heroes like yourself, Kwaku Ananse. May I call you Nancy and you call me Nelson."

"Thank you Nelson. Tell me about your life."

"Very well!"

So Nelson began:

"I was born Nelson Rolihlahla Mandela on the 18th July 1918, being fortunate to be born of the royal line of Tembu in Umthata in the Transkei of the Eastern Cape.

I was educated in a boarding school, then went on to University.

It wasn't long before I began to respond to injustices by organising a strike on the campus and was summarily expelled, so I had to make a hasty retreat to Soweto, but soon bounced back by taking a Law Degree at the University of South Africa, which helped some friends and I to establish South Africa's first black law firm.

It soon became clear to me, that my mission in life was to be an agitator against the unfairness of apartheid."

"Apartheid! What that?"

"Well Anansi! With the motto of your country being 'Out of Many, One People,' you'll be unfamiliar with the appalling scab on the back of my nation that we call apartheid, or 'being apart.'"

"Tell me more!"

"I'm sure that a black man in Jamaica wouldn't be put in jail for drinking from the same tap as a white man."

"Not in this day and age!" I stuttered in amazement.

"Well that's only one of the many humiliations that my people suffer, at the hands of a racist white minority."

I butted in:

"We have a peculiar syndrome in Trench Town, where black Jamaicans with lighter skin, can be persecuted by those of more 'pure' origin. Bob Marley used to have trouble on this account when he was growing up. His father was white you see."

"Of mixed race was he? In South Africa a mixed marriage is destined to run into serious trouble, but I've no time for such bigotry and I shall continue to fight against it. Anyway! What was I saying? Oh! yes! In 1944, we set up the African National Congress Youth League, but my activities led to me being arrested for 'treason.' That's what they called it when you fought against oppression."

"We have known that ploy here in Jamaica, when we were trying to throw off the yolk of slavery."

"I'm sorry to say that this forced me to be militant, forming a military wing, that we called the 'Spear of the Nation."

"Just like Nanny!"

"I came to be known as the 'Black Pimpernel,' because I was skilled at disguising myself, coming and going at will, but in 1964 my luck deserted me and I was thrown in jail to serve 27 years for their favoured charge of treason. Things were very harsh for my patriots and myself in the prison on Robben Island."

"Our hero Alexander Bustamante suffered some of that indignity. He would have loved to have met you, Nelson."

Nelson continued:

"Whilst I was living out my sentence, many brave people lost their lives in the struggle, but the white overlords started to realise that they couldn't hold down the nation for ever and began moves to release me from prison.

I was eventually set free early in 1990.

Since then I've been on a tour to influence world powers to apply sanctions against our white government, to persuade them to abolish the segregation of the people. That's why I'm here!

"Are you hopeful of victory?"

"If right doesn't defeat wrong eventually, there's no point in fighting, but I'll tell you this Nancy, I've learned that violence can't solve the pain. If I eventually govern, it will be with in a spirit of reconciliation, not revenge, and all men will stand side by side as equals."

"I'll pray to my Lord Nyame on your behalf."

Nelson had such a delightful smile as he said:

"Well that's enough of me. I need a cold drink after so much talking, so let me rest now whilst you tell me one of your stories."

I was proud to entertain this courageous man that evening, but I had a strange premonition that this was to be my final story.

The Gungo Peas

There was once a King, who owned much farmland.

He instructed that one of his fields be planted with gungo peas, and in no time at all, the peas grew plump and nice.

They were admired by every passer by and soon began to go missing, so the King sent one of his farm hands to guard his precious crop.

One day, as I was passing by, I asked the watchman if I could take a handful of peas home, to feed my hungry children.

"No! Anansi. Without permission from my master, I can't even let you come onto this field, never mind take away his gungo peas."

"I'll seek the King and obtain his permission."

I lied.

The next day I returned, carrying an official looking letter in my hand.

"Here's the King's permission for me to eat his peas."

I smiled as I handed it to the watchman.

"That's no good!" he protested "I can't read, you see."

"I'll read it for you then." said I and with a grand gesture, I opened the letter and in my most important voice I read out:

"To my watchman of the gungo pea field.

This is to inform you to tie my good friend

Mister Kwaku Anansi to the fattest gungo peas.

When his belly is full, let him go.

Signed by:

'...carrying an official looking letter...'

Your Mighty King."

The watchman didn't suspect a trick, tied me to the peas, waited until my belly was full, then let me go.

Soon after I left, the King apparently came to check his field and was so angry to be told that I had tricked the watchman.

"Now listen carefully you fool. I wrote no such letter. If Anansi comes to play the same trick again, just tie him up and leave him."

The next day I went back and handed the watchman the fake letter.

With a sly smile, he tied me to the peas and I began to feast.

"Mister Watchman, I've finished! You can release me now."

"Certainly not Anansi! I'm wise to your mischief. You can stay there until my master comes."

"If you don't let me go, I'll curse you."

The watchman didn't like this one little bit, but he still refused to release me.

"I won't say it again! I'm an Obeah man and if I'm not freed this very minute, I'll spit on the floor and you'll go rotten and die."

The workman shook with fear and cut me loose.

I knew now that he feared me, so the next day I took my letter and insisted that he carry out its instructions, which he did.

When my belly was full, I called for him to untie me from the peas.

"You may curse me, Anansi, but my master says that if I let you go this time he will kill me." and he ran away.

Later that evening, the King passed his field, looking for his workman, but only found me. He carted me off to his yard, tied me up to a tree, put a flat iron on the fire to get it good and hot, then went indoors.

Brer Tiger was passing by, so I took to crying in anguish.

"What happens?" asked Tiger.

"I'm going to be punished by the King, because I can't use a knife and fork, Bredda Tiger."

"You're a hopeless case, Anansi, but I'll free you and you can tie me up in your place and I'll teach this King a lesson."

I wondered what he was planning to do, but not wishing to stay around to see, I tied Tiger loosely to the tree, went into the bush and climbed a tree to see what happened.

The King came out and saw Tiger, so taking the hot iron, he shoved it in his ear.

Tiger gave a mighty roar, broke loose and rushed off into the bush, howling in pain. He saw me hiding in the tree, so he began to shake it, crying;

"Come down here you wretched spider. I'm going to eat you up."

I was frightened and began to tremble, but I began to call out to the King:

"The man you're looking for is under this tree."

Tiger galloped away.

I strolled home.

Mister Mandela. I wouldn't choose for you to be treated like Tiger.

* * * * * * *

Nelson Mandela went on to be the first black President of South Africa and to win the Nobel Peace Prize.

The A.N.C. laid down its arms in 1996, after thirty years of struggle and Nelson kept the promise that he made in my presence.

There was no revenge meted out on the white population, only a programme to bring solidarity to the nation.

One of reconciliation, confession and forgiveness.

I had a wonderful vision of Michael and Edward shaking hands at the Marley One Love Peace Concert, but this faded as it was replaced by one of gangsters prowling the streets of Kingston, killing without remorse.

The dream of Martin Luther King faded away.

Beneath a facade of democracy, life in the ghetto remained poor, making this place in Jamaica hell in heaven.

I thought back to the times when the enemies were our slave masters and the soldiers of British Imperialism.

In those days, our heroes knew where to focus their attention, but now the enemy lived within.

Black kills black.

Jamaican robs Jamaican.

Families feud over the ownership of land.

The purpose of attending a funeral is often not to show respect for a loved one, but for families to rob each other of the worldly goods of their recently departed.

In life and in death brother robs brother.

We begged and we stole, whilst Nyame and Jesus wept for their children.

As I looked back over the many hundreds of years that I've stayed close to my people, supporting them during often horrendous times, telling them stories of encouragement and stories of hope, another great sadness began to well over me.

Why do my people no longer remember my adventures?

Why do some even deny my existence and origins?

Where have I gone wrong?

Why have I failed?

* * * * * *

A great pain surges through my body, then I hear a voice calling me and I feel a familiar touch on my forehead that brings me back.

"Wake up husband! You're moaning in your sleep."

The misty clouds drift away as I roll over, open my heavy eyes, and find myself swinging on my hammock, high in the rafters of Alvan's house.

Crooky is close by my side saying:

"You worry me, dear husband. Your skin is hot and clammy."

'...Patterson calls out the army.'

I raise myself up on two elbows and look down.

Patrice and Geana are at the table, eating their breakfast of achee, salt fish and fried plantain and Winnie fusses around, hustling them along, so that they won't be late for school.

Alvan must have already left for work, for there is no sight or sound of him.

Spread out on the table is a newspaper with a headline 'WAR IN WEST KINGSTON'.

"Not again!" I gasp.

The moment that the girls set out for school and Winnie heads into the yard to do more chores, I struggle down to read the news.

The paper is dated July 24th, 2001 and as I flick over the pages I am faced with horrendous stories.

'Gunfights between security forces, police and gunmen'.

'A 14 year old boy shot dead on Bond Street'.

'More than 41 civilians attending Kingston Public Hospital with gun-shot wounds'.

'Explosives thrown at Police Command Post'.

'Policeman burnt in his car on Mountain View Avenue'.

'At least 26 persons shot dead since last Saturday'.

'Police Inspector shot dead in his car and his 9mm pistol stolen'.

'Prime Minister Patterson calls out the army.'

A story of 'the stench of unrefrigerated rotting corpses piled up two and three high in a funeral parlour in North Street'.

I swing back to the rafters, nauseated by the images portrayed.

I think of words from Marley's song Rat Race, when he sings "political violence stills your city". He sang this in the 1970's, but still it continues.

I let out a long moan of grief.

"Oh! Crooky! I do feel so weak and helpless. I do believe that I am about to die!"

"You've said that before to trick me!"

"No trick this time, Crooky! Father Nyame did warn me, just before I came to earth, that I would only exist as long as my people believed in me."

"I believe in you, husband."

"You are so dear to me, Crooky, but only my people hold the power of life and death over me."

"But what will become of me, and what of Takuma and Doshey? If you die, we die also."

"I know! I know! But our destiny lies in the hands of those who have forgotten the old ways."

I kneel down on my wondrous web, extend my arms to heaven and cry out:

"Nyame! Nyame! My Father in the Sky!

Please hear my prayer that peace may come to this nation and that I may not be forgotten.

Intervene on my behalf.

I pray that I may still continue to be the fighter for freedom and the trickster that you created to be Saviour of your Ashanti nation.

Reveal yourself and tell your children to remember my stories, so that they do not forget me.......

.... don't forget me!

.... don't forget me!

.... don't forget me!

.... don't forget me!

About the Author

David Brailsford was born in Nottingham, England in 1930.

He was educated at the High Pavement Grammar School.

Qualifying as a Psychiatric Nurse in 1955, he progressed through his profession to become a Senior Nursing Officer.

He developed a Staff In-house Training Department and worked with clients as a Registered Dramatherapist.

Now retired, he spends much of his time writing tales about Jamaican history, folk lore and fantasy.

His first book was a collection of ghost stories, entitled Jamaican Duppy Stories.

Currently working on a book of short stories about Obeah, the practice of witchcraft in Jamaica, gives him a good excuse to visit his friends and relatives in Porus, Manchester Parish, to do 'research' in the local bar.

He has three daughters and ten grandchildren and lives with his Jamaican born wife Leonie, in Nottingham, England.

She is his inspiration to write these 'old-time' stories.

About the Illustrator

John Stilgoe was born in Liverpool, England, and being surrounded by comedians, it was inevitable that he became a cartoonist interested in humorous illustration.

He graduated from the North Staffordshire Polytechnic with a BA (hons) in Fine Art and from Leicester Polytechnic with an Art Teacher's Diploma and a Post Graduate Certificate in Education.

John has taught Art and Technology in various schools and colleges and is currently Head of Art, Design and Technology in a Hinckley High School.

His cartoons and illustrations have been used in advertising, training, promotions and presentations by industry, education and private individuals, which have included TTS Education supplies, the BMW Club Journal, Clarion Magazine and the RSPCA.

In 1999, John won 1st place for a single image gag at the Leicester Festival of Comedy.

John also illustrated David's first book entitled Jamaican Duppy Stories and is currently working on other projects with him.

Since eteach.com went on line, John has been the editorial cartoonist and more of his work can be seen on-line at www.johnstilgoe.co.uk.

He lives in Nuneaton with his wife and six children.

LaVergne, TN USA
09 September 2009
157240LV00001B/17/A